An Unquenchable Fire is a story based on true events. The events that took place during the early Christian church are ones of excitement, bravery, faith, and love.

It was my goal to reinterpret, through a teenage girl's eyes, the exciting events surrounding the growth of Christianity.

Keep in mind, that because this book is a story of fact mingled with fiction, I, the writer, have taken creative liberty to introduce characters.

Perpetua's character was inspired by the story of Perpetua, who died for her faith in Carthage. Remember, Perpetua in this book is *not* the Perpetua who gave her life for her faith.

There are some scriptural references in this book, all of which are taken from the New King James Version of the Bible.

This book is based on true events; therefore, I have taken the liberty to dramatize situations that may have occurred.

I do not wish to stray from the boundaries of scripture, so there are a few scenes in the book which are not intended for younger readers.

Reader discretion is highly advised.

For now we see through a glass, darkly; but then face to face: now I know in part; but then shall I know even as also I am known.

1 Corinthians 13:12

Dedication

To my sister, Tiny, who stood by my side during the entirety of this book. Thank you for taking such enthusiasm in helping me put this book together!

And to all who desire the 'Unquenchable Fire'

Acknowledgments

I want to thank my Lord and Savior, Jesus Christ, for His wonderful gift of salvation that He offers to all who believe on Him.

I want to thank all of my wonderful editors for their help and support.

I want to thank Boo_bee, my illustrator, for the beauty she has brought to my book. God has blessed you tremendously.

And last, but never least, I want to thank my wonderful, amazing family, who supported me through the process of this book. God bless you guys!

Chapter 1

Excitement in Jerusalem

Perpetua awoke and rolled onto her back; the sunlight in her eyes made it nearly impossible to open them.

Groaning, she rolled back onto her stomach and opened her eyes. Her long brown hair fell over her shoulder as she propped herself up on her elbow.

Perpetua swung her legs over the edge of her bed, a large square- shaped bed with golden edges used only by the rich. Her deep brown eyes took in the objects around her room: her small table which held a small pitcher of water for washing her hands, a stool for putting on her sandals, and the lamp beside her bed for light.

Perpetua's eyes widened and a smile crossed her pretty face as she remembered what today was.

Perpetua's father, one of the most powerful tribunes in Jerusalem, Marcus Antonius, had given her permission to walk around the city for a day.

Since the death of the Nazarene, Jesus, the city had been incredibly stressful and quiet, and the people, not knowing what to do except follow orders from the Jewish leaders, kept themselves under control.

Marcus had been there on that awful day when the Nazarene was put to death and never wanted to hear anything about that day again.

But today is good, Perpetua thought. Calling for her servi (the roman word for slave), Perpetua got up. *Better get going before Father changes his mind,* Perpetua thought.

When Hagathe, her servi, entered the room, she smiled. "Getting ready to go already?" Hagathe said, her thick Hebrew accent coming through as she spoke.

Perpetua nodded. "I don't want Father to change his mind." Hagathe chuckled. "I don't think he would do that, Miss Perpetua." Hagathe said.

As she began to brush Perpetua's hair, Hagathe continued, "Your father is a kind and good man, and he wants to make you happy."

A short while later, Perpetua's hair was up, half of it braided into a bun on top of her hair and the other half left down and flowing. Hagathe then helped Perpetua slip on a lavender purple dress and handed Perpetua her sandals.

"Be down in time for breakfast!" Hagathe called, as she left the room. After finishing the task of putting on her shoes, Perpetua ran down the stairs into the dining hall.

Perpetua's nineteen-year-old sister, Justina, was already at the table with Father waiting for Perpetua and her little brother, Augustus. Father looked up and smiled. "Good morning, Sweetheart."

From upstairs they could hear Augustus fighting with his nursemaid, Ahinoam. "Let me go, meanie! Father will have your head! Father, Father! Help!"

Justina rolled her eyes. "Why can't he just come downstairs peaceably like the rest of us?" she asked, impatiently.

Father smiled, "He's a boy, Justina. A young four-year-old boy." Justina rolled her eyes again and sighed.

At last, the family was sitting at the table eating a pleasant breakfast of Tagenitai, a pancake type food, served with honey and dates and a small bowl of porridge.

As usual, Augustus was doing most of the talking. "My servi is so mean!" Augustus shouted. Father looked at Augustus and said, "Why do you say that Gus?" Augustus smiled mischievously.

"Because" he said mock-offendedly, "she tried to do my hair!"

Justina slammed her spoon on the table. "How is that mean?" she demanded.

Augustus just laughed and flipped his porridge bowl, with food still inside, upside down, jumped out of his chair and ran into another room.

Justina's patience had reached the breaking point. She screamed and ran after Augustus. "Come here you little pig!" Father chuckled. Perpetua smiled as she finished eating.

"Father," Perpetua said slowly. "Did the officers tell the truth a few months ago, when they said that the followers of the Nazarene stole his body?"

Marcus stopped eating. He stared at his food for a long time. "Pepi, do you remember when the cohort of officers captured the criminal, Barabbas? It was during the time when the Jewish leaders were in the process of capturing the Nazarene."

Perpetua nodded. "Yes, Father. I remember; Why?" Marcus looked her square in the eyes now. "What did I tell you when we captured him?"

Perpetua looked down. "You told me not to ask questions about him nor to mention him at all in the home."

Father nodded. "Therein lies your answer for your original question. Now you must excuse me, I have to go in and see the chief priests and the council today."

As Father walked away from the table, Perpetua wondered why things had to be so strict when it came to things that applied to the Jewish people. *Better not keep thinking about these things*, she thought to herself.

Getting up from the table, she walked into the family room where the images of four of the gods sat on a shelf.

Perpetua looked at them for a while. A feeling of dissatisfaction came over her as she thought, *Why do we worship these things? They never do anything for us any way.* She thought of asking her father about it but wisely decided against it.

Finally, she walked toward them, looked at them for a split second more. She was torn between what her conscience was telling her and what she had been taught.

Deciding to follow her conscience, Perpetua shook her head and walked out of the front door.

The air was so pleasant as she stepped out onto the street that Perpetua couldn't help but smile.

Perpetua herself didn't have any friends save her little brother, but she still felt as if she had a friend when she was in nature.

When she got to the marketplace, it was busy and bustling with merchants trying to sell their wares.

Typically, Romans wouldn't mingle with Jews unless they had to, but today was different; it was the start of the Jewish holiday, The Feast of Weeks.

People from all over the world were there and Perpetua took the time to count how many people from different countries she could see at one booth.

Ambling on through the crowded streets, she passed the Antonia Fortress, which was blocked by a wall that made up part of the temple wall.

The fortress was just barely tall enough to be seen over the wall. The fortress had been placed in the temple court to ensure that people wouldn't get riled up and do something they shouldn't.

When she got to the gate of the temple called, Beautiful, she noticed a crippled man lying there begging for coins.

Even though she was Roman, Perpetua had a soft heart. Feeling in her purse for a few coins, she walked up the steps toward the man.

She was easily recognized by her fair skin and lighter hair, but she didn't care.

When she got to the man, he seemed frightened. "Don't be afraid," she said softly, "I'm here to give you some money."

She put the coins in the man's money bowl and stood up and began to walk away.

When she got to the bottom of the stairs, she heard a commotion at the top.

Looking up she saw two averagely dressed men talking to the cripple. She heard the cripple ask them for some money and watched as one of the men turned his hands, palms up, to show the cripple that he had no money.

She heard the man say, “Friend, look at us. We don’t have any silver or gold, but we do have something.”

The cripple looked a little confused but still curious. The man continued. “In the name of Jesus Christ of Nazareth, Stand up. Walk.”

Perpetua watched as the cripple took hold of one of the other man’s hands and slowly, very slowly, began to stand up.

Soon the man was jumping up and down and praising God and telling everyone he passed how he had been healed.

Perpetua’s eyes bugged out. She followed at a distance as the two men took the now dancing man into the court that the Jews called Solomon’s Hall.

She watched as the two men stood up to speak. The one who healed the cripple was speaking.

“Men and brothers,” he began. “Why are you amazed at this? Why do you look at us as if we did this by ourselves?"

With that, the man dove into the story of the crucifixion of the Nazarene.

He began by saying, "I know that you and your leaders didn't know what you were doing, and God knows that. He is willing to forgive you if you will just repent."

The people began to shout, "We repent! We repent!"

The man went to continue speaking, when the priests and the Sadducees and the captain of the guards came out and heard what the men were teaching the people. They became livid.

The priests shouted, "Arrest them!" and the people called out, "No! leave them alone! Leave Peter and John alone!" But the priests grabbed them and took them into the council room.

As Perpetua watched, she whispered to herself, "If this is what the followers of the Nazarene can do just by speaking, who knows what they will do when they start working!

Here's what I do know, if Peter and John value their lives, they'll watch what they say.

Whatever's going to happen, it's going to be very exciting!"

Chapter 2

Getting to Know the Apostles

As Perpetua walked away from the temple, she pondered what she had seen. It didn't make any sense!

What did the man, Peter, mean when he had said that everyone there had crucified the Nazarene and that they must ask for forgiveness?

Wasn't it the Jewish leaders and the roman guards that had killed the Nazarene?

But Peter had said that *all* who had sinned had crucified Him and Jesus was alive and that he was waiting to receive those who would repent.

As she was thinking about this, she heard some women talking excitedly, their thick Hebrew accents made it slightly difficult to understand them.

"Did you hear?"

"No, what happened?"

"Peter and John are being held in custody for preaching in the temple and saying that Jesus is alive."

"No!"

"Yes! But there's something more!"

"What?"

"Five *thousand* men were added to the believer group! Just from that sermon in the temple!"

"No way!"

"Yep. That's what I heard anyway."

"Woah."

Perpetua's interest was piqued. She had to find out more about these believers.

What made them so powerful in their preaching? She had to know.

As she walked up the winding path to her house, she wondered if she should mention anything about what she saw that day.

She knew that Father would probably know about the incident already and so it would probably be best not to mention it.

When she got home, Justina was waiting for her.

“Where have you been, young lady?” Justina demanded. “Do you realize what time it is?” Perpetua shook her head. “No,” she said quietly.

Justina’s hands were now on her hips and she was shaking her head. She was quite furious.

“Perpetua, our Avus (the roman word for grandfather), King Herod, has invited us to the palace for three days. We were supposed to be there by now but we’re late because *you’re* late!”

Perpetua nodded slowly. She didn’t say anything. She simply walked by Justina and into the house.

Justina followed behind and said, "Don't you care about the fact that we're late because of you?" Perpetua turned around.

Her sister was a spitting image of their mother. The red hair. The dark eyes. The cocky attitude.

"Do you remember what Mother used to tell us before bed?" Perpetua asked. Justina nodded. "She would say, 'Don't be afraid to ask questions about what you see. You deserve an answer.' She died shortly after saying that, Pepi." Perpetua's head dropped.

"Father said he would meet us at Avus' palace." Justina said quietly.

"Do you think" Perpetua began, "that it's wrong to ask questions about sects and religions that differ from ours?"

Justina shook her head. "I think that it is good to ask questions but not to change your beliefs just because some other idea sounds better."

Soon, the three children, Justina, Perpetua, and Augustus, were sitting in the carriage headed for Herod's palace. It was a lovely trip, and it gave Perpetua a chance to think.

Perpetua's mother had been the favorite daughter of Herod. She had been raised spoiled.

Mother had been walking with her servis when she had seen Marcus, a centurion at the time, riding on a horse with officers marching behind him.

Pomona, the children's mother, had taken a special interest in Marcus and fourteen weeks after meeting him they were married. Marcus was then promoted to the rank of tribune, much to Pomona's delight.

At last, three miles later, the children arrived at their Avus's home.

Servis helped the children exit their carriage and enter the lavish palace. It was a big place, with a massive foyer and arches to greet them.

A thought dawned on Perpetua as she was escorted to her room; She could find the believers much faster now that she was in the heart of Jerusalem.

Perpetua walked into the living room of the house and breathed in the smell of her Avus's home.

She walked into the sitting room where her materteras (the roman word for maternal aunts) were chatting.

"Good evening, Matertera Fortuna." Perpetua said.

Matertera Fortuna looked up. "Good evening, darling."

The ladies were discussing the new group of believers that had sprung up since the death of the Nazarene.

"It's not smart to start something new so soon after their leader's death." Matertera Maia said cautiously, "You never know what these kinds of things can lead to. You know the government doesn't need any more stress."

After dinner, the children were getting ready for bed. Hagathe was helping Perpetua let down her hair.

"Servi?" Perpetua said quietly. Hagathe replied gently, "Yes?"

"Do you know why it is wrong to mention the new sect of believers?" Perpetua continued.

Hagathe stopped unbraiding Perpetua's hair and said slowly, "I think that your family has their reasons. You know that with every sect that arises there is bound to be something that makes it fall."

As Perpetua laid in bed, she thought about what she had seen at the temple that morning. She had to find out where the believers met.

She had to know how they preached with such influence. *How is it that such few believers have such a big influence on people?*

The next morning, Perpetua awoke and jumped out of bed. She ran downstairs and out the front door. Coming to the temple, she saw people gathered around the council steps.

"What's going on?" she asked the woman standing closest to her. The woman was a Jew and Perpetua could tell by her accent when she said, "Peter and John were held in custody all night. Right now, the council is speaking with them. We think they will be released momentarily."

Perpetua waited with the group until they saw Peter and John come out, unharmed, and smiling.

The woman met them with open arms saying, "We were worried that there would be trouble. We knew better than to anticipate anything else. Jesus said that we would be hated.

"How blessed are we to be partakers in his suffering even if it isn't very much."

Peter said, “Let’s go to the brothers and tell them what God has done for us.” “Yes.” John agreed.

The woman looked at Perpetua. “Do you want to go with us? Visitors are always welcome.”

Perpetua looked nervous. She fidgeted with the hem of her sleeve and then said, “Are you sure I will be welcome? After all I am a Roman.”

The woman smiled broadly. “Absolutely. Jesus told us that everything that we do to even the least of his followers is done to him. The least we can do is show you where we meet, in case you want to join us permanently.”

Perpetua followed the three back to the place where all of the believers met.

As they entered, the believers greeted each other and then looked at Perpetua.

“Is she one of us?” a tall man asked. The woman nodded. “I asked her if she wanted to see where we met in case she decides to join us."

A man in the corner said, "Mary, we are grateful that you've found a new friend to join us."

Mary took Perpetua to meet all of the other believers. After meeting everyone, Peter told the story of their boldness in the council. "We told them, is it better to God for us to listen to you or to listen to Him? You get to choose what you want. But we cannot help but speak of the things that we saw and the things we heard. They then threatened us and released us."

All of the believers then got down on their knees and prayed. They praised God for His protection and then prayed for boldness, that they would be able to stand when trial and persecution arose, knowing that they must suffer for Jesus' name.

As the believers were praying, the building began to shake. Perpetua saw as each of the brothers and sisters became filled with the Holy Spirit and they went out and started preaching with the boldness that they had asked for.

A few days later, in early hours of the morning, when Perpetua returned to see the believers, she saw a lot of people meeting with the believers. She found Mary putting food in a basket and asked her what was going on. Mary said quickly, "The believers are coming together to help one another. Like a big family, nothing that we have is our own. We share everything."

Perpetua looked over at where Peter was sitting and saw people coming with their money and giving it to him. "What are *they* doing?" she asked.

Joanna, another of the followers of Jesus and wife of one of Herod's servants, said, "They're giving money to help those followers who are less fortunate and out of work." Perpetua nodded slowly. *These people take better care of their own people than Caesar claims he does for us!*

She stayed with the believers for the rest of the day, watching the gifts that were brought in and helping put together gifts for others. Finally, though, it was time for Perpetua to go.

As Perpetua walked home that evening she thought carefully. The believers took care of one another. Even when their leaders were facing death, the believers had faith that all would be well. She didn't understand it.

Slowly but steadily, the hand of God started working in this young girl. She didn't know it, but the God of the Jews had a lot planned for her!

Chapter 3

To Test the Spirit

When Perpetua got home, she noticed that everyone was there, waiting for her. She smiled and said, "Good evening, family." Perpetua's father glared at her. She started feeling nervous. "Is something the matter?" she asked quietly.

Matertera Fortuna looked at Perpetua and then said, very slowly, "Yes… you have been gone *all* day, my dear." Perpetua looked outside. It was true. The sun was now setting and when she had left, the sundial had shown the time being eight.

"My apologies, dear family. I lost track of time," Perpetua said softly. Justina sighed dramatically. "You lost track of time?" She nearly shouted. Perpetua looked at the ground as Justina continued. “You’ve been so distracted by whatever’s going on in town that you can’t seem to keep anything in your normal life straight!”

Just then, Marcus broke into the conversation. “Yes, what has been going on in town that keeps grabbing at your attention?” he asked authoritatively. Perpetua went to answer when Augustus ran in.

“Father,” Gus began, but Father brushed him off as he waited for Perpetua’s answer. “Father!” Augustus said earnestly. Marcus straightened and looked down at his young son. “What does it look like I’m doing, Son?” he asked Gus. Gus looked up innocently and said, “It looks like you’re not doing anything of terribly great importance.”

Marcus’ anger had almost reached the breaking point. Trying very hard to restrain his anger toward his son, Marcus said slowly but emphatically, “Go sit down for dinner son. I’ll hear what you have to say in there.” Motioning for

Perpetua to go to her room, Father turned and went into the dining room.

In her room, Perpetua could hear the excited chatter around the table. She knew that Gus had probably said something hilarious and wished she could be there. She wondered if tonight she would be up late, talking with her father and her materteras about why she was always gone. She knew too that Justina would probably join the conversation just to get angry with her.

Two hours later, when Gus and Justina were sent to bed, Father called Perpetua out of her room. When she got downstairs, Materteras Fortuna and Maia were waiting.

"Perpetua," Matertera Fortuna said. "Will you answer a question for me?" Perpetua nodded slowly. Matertera Fortuna said very emphatically, "Where do you go when you are in town?"

Perpetua took a deep breath. "I go around town and I watch the different things that happen there." Matertera

Maia had a look of understanding and concern all at the same time.

Father spoke up. “Perpetua, are you telling me that for the past three days you have been wandering around town doing nothing but watching the things that happen there?” Perpetua nodded again.

Father stood up and started pacing. “Pepi, you know you are a terrible liar, right?” he asked slowly. Perpetua said softly, “Yes, Father.” “Then what are you doing when you go to town?” Father said, his voice rising a little.

Perpetua knew that if she told her father the truth, it could result in him requiring her to stay home indefinitely. She also knew that if she didn’t tell him the truth, he would find out sooner or later.

Taking another deep breath, she said, “I go, and I meet with the followers of the Nazarene,” she began. As she did, she could feel her Father and both of her aunts, stiffen. She continued, “They help and encourage one another. They teach that the Nazarene, Jesus, is alive and that..." She could get no farther. Marcus had heard plenty.

Swift as an arrow, his hand landed firmly against her cheek. Perpetua could feel tears rise in her eyes as the stinging, tingling sensation echoed across her face. She heard her aunts jump, startled by what had just happened, and then start questioning Marcus.

"What was that for?"

"You know she didn't deserve that!"

Summoning all of her courage, Perpetua said boldly, "Jesus Christ is alive, and he is working through his followers," Another slap followed. "Jesus is risen, and He has started a work, a flame, that can never be quenched!"

Now her Matertera Fortuna joined in hitting her. Still, Perpetua spoke. "Jesus Christ is the Messiah; He has set His people free! He emboldens His followers to do what he says.

That's all I wanted to find out! That's the only reason I leave at the early hours of the morning, to find out how and why Jesus' followers are making such a radical change and…"

She never finished. A blow from Justina's fist knocked her unconscious.

When she awoke, Perpetua was in a small room that she didn't recognize. She looked around the small room and smiled. Now she knew where she was. The smell of Mary and Joanna's cooking made up the aroma of the room.

Mary came in just then. "Good morning, sweet girl!" She greeted Perpetua. Perpetua smiled and returned the greeting.

Shortly after eating, Perpetua asked Mary, "Who brought me here?" Mary smiled and said, "Andrew. He found you at the gate, 'Beautiful', and then brought you here. James and Matthias helped me make this room comfortable and Joanna put you in bed."

Perpetua looked confused. “I was arguing with my family over why I came to visit you all so much and they were hitting me and then suddenly everything went dark.”

Mary shrugged. “I don’t know what to tell you.” Perpetua closed her eyes and sighed, “I think I’m safe now.”

Mary laughed. “As soon as you’re ready we can use your help,” Mary said, as she left the room.

As the days’ passed, Perpetua helped the believers where she could. Since she was rich, Perpetua had never been taught how to work with her hands, but now, Mary, Joanna, and Susanna, another follower, were teaching her how to work and clean.

Perpetua had thought of going home but the believers had told her that it would probably be best not to.

A few weeks after Perpetua had moved in with the believers, she was watching Peter collecting money for the poorer believers.

She had seen a certain man, Barnabas by name, come and give generous donations to the believers. Often she was moved to tears at how generous he really was.

One day, though, she watched as a man came to Peter and said, “Peter, my wife and I have thought that we should sell a piece of property and give the profits to you to deal it out to those who are unfortunate enough to not have homes.” Peter smiled, “Thank you, Ananias, may God bless you.”

A few days later, Ananias returned to give the money to Peter. As he walked up, though, something seemed a little off to Perpetua.

“Good morning, Peter.” Ananias said. Peter smiled, cheerfully and said, “Good morning, Ananias.” “Peter,” Ananias began, “You know we were trying to sell our land. Well, it…it didn’t bring in as much as we thought it would.

It did bring in *some* money so here you go."

Peter looked at the bag of money sitting on the table he then looked back up at Ananias.

Finally, he spoke. "Ananias, why has Satan filled your heart to lie to the Holy Spirit and keep back part of the money from the land for yourself?

"While it was still in your name was it not your own to do with as you thought best? And after you sold it, was the money not yours to do with whatever you wanted to?

"Why have you thought to do this thing? You have not lied to men. You have lied to God."

Just as Peter finished talking, Ananias fell dead at his feet. The women gasped and the men stood back. Peter then said, "Young men, please take his body and bury it." The boys then picked up Ananias' body and carried it out.

Three hours later, Saphira, Ananias' wife came in, looking for her husband. Peter, seeing her, asked, "Saphira, did you sell your land for this amount here?"

Saphira took one look at it and said, "Yes, that's all we got for it." Peter sighed sadly and replied saying, "Why did you both agree to test the Spirit of the Lord? Look! The young men who have carried out your husband and buried him are standing right there and they will carry you out, too."

On hearing this, Saphira froze. She got a blank look in her eyes. Then she fell down, dead at Peter's feet.

Susanna gasped, Mary blinked, Joanna was frozen stiff, and Perpetua covered her open mouth with her hand.

The young men came in again and picked up Saphira's body and placed it in a neat grave beside her husband.

In the days and weeks that followed, fear came on everyone for miles around. The disciples again picked up preaching and healing.

They did many miracles and when people would ask how they did it, the believers would tell them about Jesus.

A few weeks after the Ananias and Saphira incident, Perpetua went to Peter and asked, “How do I join the group of believers?” Peter smiled and said, “I see you want to join us permanently.”

Perpetua smiled broadly and nodded quickly. Peter said, “Then all you need to do is accept Jesus Christ as the Savior and Messiah and then we will baptize you into the faith that Jesus has given us.” Perpetua said, “Peter, I would like to be baptized.” Peter smiled and nodded.

A week later, Perpetua was standing in a river, with the disciple John standing beside her.

John said to those on shore, “Friends, you can see that our group grows daily and as you can see, God is sending us young people such as Perpetua to help carry on the work He entrusted to us."

Turning to Perpetua, John said, "My dear, do you believe that Jesus Christ is the Son of God and that He is the Messiah?" Perpetua smiling, said, "I do. I believe that Jesus Christ is the Son of God."

John smiled at her and then said, "Then, I baptize you in the name of the Father, of the Son, and of the Holy Spirit, Amen."

As she went under the water, Perpetua prayed, *'Lord I am Yours. Use me for Your service. Help me to never look back on my decision!'*

Chapter 4

Prison Escape

As Perpetua broke up through the water, she could feel the air greet her face. She heard the believers on shore cheering and when she opened her eyes she saw John smiling down at her. She hugged him and ran onto shore where Susanna was waiting with open arms.

Perpetua hugged Susanna and Mary and then turned to the other believers who each took turns hugging her and praying with her.

Perpetua suddenly heard a shrill screech come from Joanna. Looking over at Joanna, Perpetua saw the high priest and the Sadducees standing a few feet away from her.

A few seconds behind the Jewish leaders, a centurion, and his soldiers arrived.

Perpetua leaned into Matthew to keep from passing out. Matthew asked, "Are you ok?" All Perpetua could do was nod.

Matthew motioned for Thaddaeus and Matthias to come and help him.

"What's wrong?" Thaddaeus asked. Matthew said, "We need to get Perpetua out of here. We need to hide her somewhere she'll be safe."

Matthias looked confused. "Ok, but why?" he asked slowly. Matthew said carefully, "I'll explain that after we get her out of danger."

While Matthew was talking, the high priest spoke up and said, "By order of the council for the bettering of our people, you are all under arrest." With that, the soldiers arrested all of them including Perpetua.

The apostles and Perpetua were carried off to the common prison and were locked up.

While inside the cell, they all discussed what a blessing it was, that they had gotten through Perpetua's baptism without interruption.

As they were talking, Philip said, "Let's sing." So, sing they did. They sang into the night and also prayed.

In the very early hours of the morning a bright light filled the cell. Perpetua was awakened by Simon, who was once a zealot.

"What is it?" Perpetua said sleepily. Simon said, "Look!" Looking, Perpetua saw a figure in the light. She couldn't recognize it, but she felt safe.

She heard Bartholomew and Thomas whisper, "An angel!" Then the angel spoke, "Go into the temple and preach to the people."

The apostles followed the angel out the first gate then into the court. Finally, they were directed to the temple. As the angel vanished from their sight, Perpetua thought, '*Woah! I just saw an angel!*'

As the believers filed into the temple, Perpetua held back. "What's wrong?" James the Just asked.

Perpetua said, "I'm not Jewish. I will not be allowed in." James smiled. "You're one of us now. It doesn't matter where you've come from, you're one of the believers."

Walking into the temple, the believers started preaching about Jesus.

A few hours later, the priest's captain and his officers came into the temple and saw the believers teaching the people. Quickly, the guards came and took the believers into the council.

In the council room, the high priest, Caiaphas, asked them, "Did we *not* strictly tell you not to teach in this name? Look! You have filled *all* Jerusalem with your doctrine and intend to bring the Nazarene's blood on us!"

All of the apostles looked at the council and Peter said, "We ought to obey *God* rather than men.

"The God of our fathers raised up Jesus, who you murdered by crucifying on a cross.

"God has raised Jesus to His right hand to be our Prince and Savior, to give repentance to Israel and forgiveness of sins.

"And we are his witnesses to these things and so is the Holy Spirit, whom God has given to those who obey him."

As Peter finished, the council became enraged. They started planning to kill the believers when a Pharisee named Gamaliel stood up and said, "I wish to say something."

Since Gamaliel was a respected man, the council quieted down and said, "Yes, rabbi?" Gamaliel nodded. "First, send these people outside for a little while and I will continue."

Caiaphas motioned for the guards to take the believers out for a little while.

After the believers were outside, Gamaliel continued. "Men of Israel, be careful what you intend on doing to these people.

"A little while ago there was a man, Theudas by name, who rose up claiming to be someone that the people should follow. About four hundred men joined him and a short while after he rose up, he was killed by the Romans.

"After that, another man, Judas of Galilee, rose up and had *many* followers. He too died and those who followed him scattered away.

"I say all this to tell you, leave these people alone. If what they teach is of themselves it will dissipate. But if this work *is* of God, you will not be able to overthrow it, otherwise you will find yourself fighting against God Himself!"

The council looked around at each other. Then, Caiaphas spoke. "We agree with your advice, brother Gamaliel. But, we cannot let them go without some sort of punishment."

At this, Annas, Caiaphas' father-in-law, said, "Let us send for the apostles and have them whipped. Then we will command them *never* to speak in the name of Jesus again."

So, they called the believers to the council room again. The priests had them walked out to the courtyard and said to the guards, "Whip them!"

Perpetua froze. She had never seen anyone be whipped before. She watched as, two at a time, the apostles were taken to the whipping block to be flogged.

She winced every time the whip struck down on the men's backs and tried to hold back the tears when it came time for Mary and Joanna to be flogged.

Finally, it was her turn. As she walked up with Susanna, she couldn't bear to see one of her closest friends be beaten right beside her. At age sixteen, Perpetua had seen a lot, but never had she felt such peace about getting wounded for the God she now loved.

One by one, the blows came. The first one, stinging Perpetua's left shoulder. The second, scraping the entire right side of her body. The third, making its definite mark on her once smooth back.

On and on it went. When it finally stopped, the blood of the apostles was on the ground, the first of many puddles that would be made by this group.

As the believers left, helping those who were more hurt, they praised God for the honor that they had, to be sufferers in the same suffering that Jesus was. They sang songs of triumph and encouraged one another in the faith.

Needless to say, the believers did not stop preaching in the temple. They went, every day, and preached to the people gathering there.

One day, as Perpetua was picking up some food from the market, she noticed that there was a woman following her.

Turning to her, Perpetua said, "Can I help you, miss?" The woman nodded. "I need to speak with you, young one."

Perpetua motioned for the alley where the woman took off her hood and Perpetua saw it was her Matertera, Maia.

"Matertera Maia! What are you doing here?" Matertera Maia smiled and said, "I've come to dissuade you from joining with the believer group."

Perpetua smiled and said firmly but still kindly, "You're too late. I've already joined them."

Matertera Maia nodded slowly. "I understand. We can take everything back, though. What your father did, what happened at the house the last you were there. We can take it all back and start over."

Perpetua nodded. Maybe it was a good idea. Maybe her father's anger had cooled down enough to return home.

Then she thought of the fact that she had just joined the faith and she remembered the fact that her father would want nothing to do with that faith.

"Hmm." Perpetua said, hand resting gently on her chin. "Matertera Maia?"

Matertera Maia looked at Perpetua. "Yes?" she said. "Was it you who took me to the gate, 'Beautiful', where the followers found me?"

Matertera Maia nodded. "Yes. Yes it was." Perpetua looked around. "Can you guarantee my safety if I return home?" Perpetua asked quietly.

Matertera Maia said, "Of course!" Perpetua nodded. "Ok. I'll go home with you then."

At home, everything was quiet. No one wanted to speak with her.

Later that evening, Father asked Perpetua to come downstairs to talk with him and the materteras. Perpetua was skeptical.

She knew what had happened the last time she had gone downstairs when her father had called her.

Finally, though, going against her better judgment, she went downstairs to talk with her family.

When she got into the family room, her father was there waiting for her. "Are you part of the believers now?" he asked bluntly. Perpetua looked him square in the eyes. "Yes I am." she said bravely.

A pain that was all too familiar to her, struck her in the face. "Do you believe in a dead Messiah, then?" It was a trick question, and Perpetua knew it.

"No, Father. I believe in a risen, alive Messiah." Another slap followed. "Are you forsaking your family to follow this ridiculousness?"

Perpetua looked at her two aunts and at her father and said, “If following my belief and obeying my God is forsaking my family, then yes, I am forsaking my family!”

Marcus’ anger flared and one after another, slaps hit Perpetua.

She turned and ran as fast as she could out of the house. When she arrived in the street she stopped and caught her breath.

It was official. Perpetua Antonius was no longer allowed in her father’s house, and she liked that.

Now that she was free of her father, she had the freedom to follow her beliefs as freely as she chose.

Father in heaven, you are my only father now. My only family is the believers. As long as I live they will *be my family and I will serve you, come what may.*

Chapter 5

Stephan

It had been a few weeks since Perpetua's decision to leave her father's home, when discontentment aroused in the Hellenists (Greek speaking Jews).

Since the church had been multiplying to such a great number, the Hellenists were complaining that their widows were not being fed in the daily distribution of food.

The twelve apostles, Peter, Andrew, James, John, Philip, Thomas, Matthew, James the Just, Thaddaeus, Simon, Matthias, and Bartholomew, got the fellow believers together and told them, "It's not something we really want to do, to leave off preaching to serve tables instead.

“In this case, brothers, and sisters, look in your midst and find seven men that have a *good* reputation, who are full of the Holy Spirit, and have wisdom.

“Find these men and they will be the ones in charge of taking care of your widows. We will keep ourselves dedicated to praying for and ministering to the people in Jerusalem.”

Everyone thought it was a good idea. So, the followers chose from among themselves, Stephan, a man who was full of faith and the Holy Spirit, Philip, Prochorus, Nicanor, Timon, Parmenas, and Nicolas.

When the believers finished choosing, they brought the seven to the disciples and had them pray over the chosen men.

After the appointing of the deacons, the disciples were able to make the word of God spread over a large portion of Jerusalem. *Many* were added to the growing church, including a pharisee named Nicodemus and others.

Perpetua enjoyed helping with the different people that would come for help.

She assigned herself as Stephan's personal helper so she could find out more about him and so she could help more people.

The two were traveling to see a shut-in believer one day, so, Perpetua got the chance to ask more about Stephan.

"What is it like to heal so many people, Stephan?" Stephan smiled down at her. "At first, it's a little shocking. After that, though, you just have to keep remembering that you're helping people for God and that everything that you're doing isn't coming from you at all, it's coming from God."

Perpetua nodded. "Was it weird the first time you healed someone?" she asked.

Stephan smiled and nodded. "Yes. It was crazy. I could barely believe it. But then I remembered the fact that Jesus had promised us the Holy Spirit, He gave us the power to do many miracles but, we must remember that it's not us doing the miracle. We must remember that it's the Holy Spirit."

Perpetua smiled at his words. They gave her comfort and knowledge. She knew that the people had chosen well in appointing Stephan.

When they arrived at the woman's home, they saw what could barely be considered a shed.

Entering, Perpetua saw dirty dishes scattered all over the floor. The house looked like it had never been swept.

Stephan found the woman, in bed, asleep. Seeing her crippled hands, Stephan felt sorry for her.

Perpetua asked, "Should I start cleaning her house?" Stephan nodded quickly and said, "Yes. We need to get this place cleaned up for her."

Perpetua, now quite skilled with a broom and a washcloth, began cleaning the house.

Stephan was in the woman's room praying for her.

An hour later, Perpetua came into the room, having finished cleaning the house.

Stephan asked, "Is everything clean and orderly?" Perpetua said, "Yes. Everything is where is should be, and it looks more like a house now."

Stephan chuckled, lightly. "We should wake her up then."

Shaking the woman, gently, Stephan said, "Miss?"

The woman yawned sleepily. Looking up and seeing Stephan, the woman jumped up and said, "Oh! I am so sorry! My house is a mess! I-I-I haven't been able to clean it because of my poor hands. I-I-I…"

Stephan gently shook his head. “It’s ok. Everything’s clean now.”

The woman looked around. Shock and surprise showed on her face. “Oh! Oh my! Did you do this?” she asked Stephan. “No,” Stephan said. “My young friend did.”

Perpetua smiled. The woman walked to her. Taking Perpetua’s hands in her crippled worn ones, she said, “God be praised! The Lord is teaching the youth to serve Him! Thank you, child!” Perpetua’s smile broadened.

Stephan took the woman’s hands and said, “Do you want your hands to be healed?”

The woman said, “Yes! Yes, please!” Stephan smiled and said, “Do you believe that God can heal you?”

The woman said, “Yes! I believe!” Stephan said, “Then, in the name of Jesus Christ, be healed!”

Perpetua watched as the woman’s scrunched up hands slowly relaxed and stretched out perfectly straight. The woman's eyes filled with tears and she turned and hugged Stephan.

Perpetua never grew tired of seeing someone be healed.

As Stephan and Perpetua walked home, Perpetua asked, "Do you enjoy healing people, Stephan?" Stephan smiled. "I enjoy every minute of it." he said. Perpetua smiled, too.

When they got into town, it was around twelve. Stopping by one of the booths, Stephan purchased a little lunch for the two of them. Sitting down on a wall nearby, they ate their lunch.

"Stephan?"

"Yes?"

"Do you ever get worried that the religious leaders will try to kill you?"

"Sometimes."

"If they did take you, what would you say?"

"I would probably defend my faith the best I could."

As the two walked back to the building where the believers met, how could they guess, that in just a few days, something terrible would test their faith in the God they loved and served.

A couple days later, as Perpetua and Stephan were finishing their checkup rounds (they would check on the different believers to make sure they were doing ok), they were stopped by some members of the Synagogue of the Freedmen.

The men started talking with Stephan. This talking soon turned into arguing. Perpetua could tell, by the look in their eyes, they meant no good for Stephan.

They tried to trip him up by their questions, but Stephan was so full of wisdom that the men could not refute what he was saying. They finally left him alone, much to Perpetua's relief.

A few days after this, some men surrounded Stephan and Perpetua again. The men said to the crowd that had gathered, “We have heard him say blasphemy against the prophet, Moses and against God Himself!”

The people became enraged and started crowding around Stephan. Perpetua watched, as the elders and the scribes shoved through the crowd and grabbed Stephan and took him to the council.

Perpetua ran to catch up with the council members. When she got to the council doors, they were slammed in her face. Unable to see what was going on inside, she ran to go get the disciples for help.

Stephan, inside the council room, was facing angry priests. False witnesses were called up to say what they needed to.

The first one said, “This man doesn’t stop speaking blasphemous words against God and the temple!” The second one said, “We have heard him say that Jesus of Nazareth will destroy the temple and change the laws that Moses delivered to us!”

The council was like lava. Looking at Stephan, they saw, not the face of a man, but the face of peace, like the face of an angel.

Quietly, Stephan stepped forward to begin his testimony.

Perpetua ran to the meeting house to try and get help for Stephan. Seeing Simon, she ran to tell him what had happened.

“Simon!” Perpetua called. “Yes?” he replied. “Simon! It’s Stephan! He’s in trouble!”

Simon looked concerned. “What kind of trouble?” Perpetua, out of breath, tried to keep talking as best she could.

“The kind where the entire council grabs him and takes him away and is probably interrogating him.”

Simon quickly put on his sandals and called for Joanna.

"Joanna, Stephan's in danger. We need to hurry. Get bandages and vinegar. Go! Hurry! Time is of the essence!"

Joanna packed a small bag of medical supplies and called Mary, Susanna, James, Matthias, and Matthew.

Quickly, the eight of them, hurried to the council. When they got there, they saw a massive crowd surrounding the council doors.

"What's going on?" James asked a man standing nearby. The man turned and said cruelly, "The criminal has been given the death sentence. He was telling the council of our history but then he told the leaders that they had killed God's Son."

Softening slightly, the man continued, "When he said that, the council became so angry they looked like a storm on the ocean.

"The man's face though... it was like nothing that I can understand. He stood still for a little while and then looked up to the roof.

"He said, 'Look! I see the heavens opened and the Son of Man sitting at the right hand of God!'

"Then, the council became even angrier. They put their hands over their ears and screamed.

"Right now, they're trying to push him out of the council room. Look! Here he comes now!"

It was true. The anger Perpetua saw in the council members eyes was pure evil.

They pushed and shoved Stephan toward the outside of the city. Perpetua ran to Stephan. "What are they going to do to you?" Perpetua said, over the roar of the mob. Stephan looked at Perpetua, sadly.

"Blessed are those who are persecuted for righteousness sake, for theirs *is* the kingdom of heaven. I know my Savior."

Perpetua looked at Stephan. "No!" she shouted. "God forbid this to happen!" Stephan looked lovingly at her. "You have to help keep the body of believers growing, Perpetua."

As the mob surged by, Perpetua struggled to stay near Stephan, who had become a very close friend to her.

"Stephan!" Perpetua screamed. Stephan looked at her again. "Pray that God won't let this happen! God will hear! Pray!"

Stephan looked at her tenderly. "I pray that this cup will pass from me. But. Not my will, but His be done." Perpetua followed as the crowd pushed Stephan.

The crowd arrived where there was a massive pile of evil looking stones.

Pushing Stephan to the ground, the people gave their coats to a young man, named Saul, while they all picked up big rocks.

One by one as Stephan looked in the eyes of the leaders he read his fate.

The first rock hit him square on his forehead. Stephan reached up to feel the blood as another rock hit him in his ribs.

Coughing, he tried to pick himself up off the ground. Just then another rock hit his cheek, throwing his balance off.

His face was now a bleeding mess as he looked into the sky and said, "Lord, receive my spirit!"

Perpetua, who had fallen quite behind the crowd, ran up just then. "Stephan!" she screamed. "No! No, no, no!"

She watched as his body became beaten unrecognizable. "Stephan!" She screamed again. Stephan looked at her. "His will, not mine," he whispered to her. The rocks kept flying.

Getting himself to his knees, he cried out, "Lord! Don't hold this sin to their charge!"

As he said this, Perpetua watched as he leaned over, and with his final breath, smiled, and breathed his last. Joanna and the men rushed over with the bandages for Stephan.

"No!" Perpetua cried. She watched as the crowd died away and carelessly walked back into the city.

Running over to Stephan, she saw his smile and wept bitterly. She looked into the sky and screamed, "Why?! How could this be Your will? He trusted you!"

Torn and weeping, Perpetua thought, *How is this possible? Is this what I'm going to have to deal with serving you? I promised I would serve you no matter what, but this is* hard! *Your will, God, not mine. Help me to always remember that.*

Chapter 6

Saul, Problems, and a Wedding

Matthew, James, Simon, and Matthias, picked up Stephan's body.

Tenderly, they carried it home where they wrapped him in cloth and made ready to take him to his grave.

Perpetua couldn't watch. She had been so close to Stephan that it felt like her heart had been ripped out of her.

She followed from a distance as the apostles and other believers carried Stephan to his grave.

When they got to his place of burial, a few devout believers dug the grave and placed Stephan's body in it. As the last shovel full of dirt was placed on the grave, everyone wept.

Peter stepped forward and said a few comforting words, after which everyone, save Joanna, Mary, and Perpetua, left.

"Are you ok?" Mary asked, gently. Perpetua nodded, still shaking with tears. Joanna's hand rested on Perpetua's shoulder as she said, "He's resting. Praise God." Perpetua looked at the grave. She shook as she wept.

As she was finally making her way home, she noticed that flowers were blooming. She smiled sadly.

On arriving home, she noticed a group of roman servis with a rich carriage parked outside the meeting house.

Looking at the different servis, Perpetua recognized two of them.

The first was Sharon, one of Justina's personal servis. The second one that she recognized was Nehushta, Justina's hired Jewish spy.

Quickly understanding that Justina was probably looking for her, Perpetua ran inside to find her sister.

Finding Justina talking with Mary, she quietly entered the room.

Turning, Justina saw Perpetua. For the first time, that Perpetua could remember, Justina smiled at her.

"Good day, sister." Justina said warmly. It startled Perpetua at first, but she returned the greeting. "Good day, *soror.*" (Soror is the roman word for sister). "I have some very exciting news!" Justina was about to burst.

Perpetua drew back. She was still shaken up by the events of the past two days and she didn't want to have her heart broken even more.

She knew that Justina probably was trying to get her to come home and whatever her plan was, Perpetua was nervous.

"Pepi, do you remember that officer we met a year ago?" Justina asked.

Perpetua nodded. It had been almost a year since Perpetua had joined the believers, but she did still remember.

The officer's name was Julius Marci. He was a tall, handsome man who stood at five feet ten inches.

He had very dark hair that was kept short to fit under his helmet. His eyes were a light color blue.

It almost felt like you were looking into the sky when you looked in his eyes. Perpetua stifled a slight laugh. She knew her sister had had her eye on him.

Remembering that Justina was still there, Perpetua nodded her response.

Justina giggled excitedly. "Well, he and father have been talking and it's finally happening!" Perpetua looked confused.

"I'm sorry, sister. I can't understand what you're trying to tell me." Perpetua said, terribly confused.

Justina giggled again. "I'm getting married! I'm getting married! I am getting *married*!"

Perpetua raised her eyebrows and chuckled, "I can see that you're excited!"

Justina grabbed her hands, startling her. "You *have* to come home with me! Help me get ready for my wedding!"

Perpetua was apprehensive. It had only been about a year since the incident of her family beating her. She really didn't want to go through that again.

Now that she was about to turn seventeen, she felt as if she had grown up with her friends, the believers. Sighing, Perpetua looked up at Justina.

Justina was pretty tall, around five feet eight inches. Perpetua took after their mother, standing at a short height of five feet three inches.

"Justina," she began. "I know you feel sorry for what happened a year ago, but I cannot come home with you." She could feel Justina stiffen.

"I know you want to make everything right; you always have.

"I just know that if I come home I won't be accepted, as you seem to think I will be."

Justina's face grew red. "I came here to bring you *home*! I came, not to ask you to come home, but to force you to come home, if need be.

I have told everyone that you would be an honored guest at my wedding. They all anticipate you to be there!" Justina screamed.

Perpetua looked down. How well she remembered her sister's fiery temper!

When she picked her head back up, it was met with a painful, stinging, smack. Memories came flooding back from a year ago.

Perpetua looked at Justina. “I’m sorry if I’ve offended you in any way. I understand it was just your temper and I forgive you.”

Justina’s anger was overflowing. She stalked outside, and in her anger, whipped both of her servis, and rode angrily away.

“It’s okay, Perpetua.” Mary said, gently. “You did the right thing.”

A few days later, when she was walking around market, Perpetua saw a group of pharisees walking past. She saw there was a young pharisee, around thirty years old, leading them.

“Who’s that?” she asked Nahum, the booth manager (who also happened to be Susanna’s husband).

Nahum looked up. “Oh.” he said, accent thick as ever. “That’s Saul of Tarsus. He’s one of the instigators of Stephan’s execution.”

Perpetua’s eyes got wide, as she turned away from the group. “Very interesting." she said, hoping not to draw attention to herself.

She knew that on the day of Stephan's death, she had made herself very obvious.

Knowing that Saul had been there, she didn't want him to see her and remember her rash behavior.

Arriving back where the apostles lived, Perpetua noticed a group of believers standing outside.

Going up to them she saw Chuza, Joanna's husband, Joanna, and Bartholomew, talking very seriously.

"Is something wrong?" Perpetua asked. Joanna nodded. "The pharisee, Saul, has been given permission, by the religious leaders, to hunt down and imprison the believers."

Perpetua gasped softly. "Who has he taken?" she asked quickly.

Chuza shook his head and shrugged his shoulders. “We don’t rightly know.” he said.

Just then, Thomas ran up to the group. “Saul of Tarsus…he…he…he’s captured Susanna and Nahum!” he breathed out.

Perpetua’s eyes got huge. “Susanna? Nahum? I just saw them!” she said.

Thomas nodded. “Apparently,” he continued, catching his breath, “He has secretly taken others as well. Rachel and Malachi, along with their six children and other family members; Tehilim and Iyov, too. And now Susanna and Nahum.”

“We need to be prepared for the worst.” Chuza said, cautiously.

Joanna nodded. “I completely agree,”

A few days had passed since Saul had kidnapped Susanna and Nahum and the believers were trying to figure out a way to get them back.

While walking down the street that passed the Temple, Perpetua heard the sounds of groaning and moaning.

Quickly darting into the temple, she saw two people at the whipping post being flogged.

Standing nearby was Saul of Tarsus with a soldier standing next to him.

Perpetua gasped and ran as far away as she could, with hot tears pouring down her face, when she noticed who it was being flogged and who the officer standing beside Saul was.

The first two individuals were Susanna and Nahum, receiving the leader's 'Thirty-Nine Lashes' (because the Jews knew that forty lashes with a whip could kill a man, they lowered the number by one).

The third individual was Julius Marci. Her sister's fiancée.

Finding Andrew at home mending a sandal, Perpetua took the time to relay to him what she had seen at the temple. Andrew nodded his head in understanding and beckoned for her to come closer.

“Can you forgive Saul for what he is doing to our friends, Perpetua?” Andrew asked, very gently. Perpetua nodded slowly.

“I don’t want to. But I will choose to.” she said.

“Andrew?” she said, quietly.

Andrew looked up at her and said, “Yes?”

“Do you know anything about Saul of Tarsus?”

Andrew stopped mending the shoe. “A little.” he said after a while.

“Anything I might want to know?” she said, curiously.

Andrew chuckled. “Umm. I know he was a tent maker with his father for a while.

“From what I hear, he left Tarsus to come here to be a Pharisee.”

Perpetua was taking in all the information. “Keep going!” she urged.

Andrew smiled. “They say, he is the sharpest pharisee they have had in a very long time.

“He follows the law to the letter, he prays, and fasts multiple times a week.”

“Is that all?” Perpetua asked.

Andrew nodded. “That’s all I know anyway.”

That night, Perpetua lay awake thinking of the man, Saul. *What kind of a man would serve God so much he would be willing to hurt his followers?*

A short time later, while Perpetua was walking home, a hand reached out, grabbed her, and pulled her into an alley.

Screaming from being startled, Perpetua turned around to see Matertera Fortuna.

“What are you doing here?” Perpetua demanded.

Matertera Fortuna smiled, snobbishly, “I’ve come to fix your broken mind, child.”

Perpetua was confused. “Broken mind?” she asked her aunt.

Matertera Fortuna nodded. “What would possess you to completely miss your own sister’s wedding?” she shouted at Perpetua.

“Was that today?” Perpetua asked.

Matertera Fortuna rolled her eyes, just like Justina would have. “Yes, it was!”

Perpetua shook free of her aunt’s grasp. “I told her I wouldn’t be there. She knew.”

Fortuna looked shocked. “What? Why in the whole of earth would you miss your *oldest* sister’s wedding to a soon to be commander? she shouted.

Perpetua shook her head. “I cannot attend something that I completely disagree with.” she said politely.

Matertera Fortuna glowered at her and then said, “This is not the last you have heard of this situation, Perpetua!” as she marched away.

When Perpetua got home (home was now wherever the apostles were living), she saw Julius at the door arresting some of the believers who had come to pray with the apostles.

Observing the situation carefully, Perpetua ambled her way around the back where the apostles were scurrying out to get away.

“What’s going on?” Perpetua whispered to John. John grabbed her hand and nearly dragged her behind him.

“John?” Perpetua asked, again.

When they finally stopped to catch their breath, John held his finger up to his mouth, “Shh.”

Listening carefully, she could hear Peter and Matthew discussing where everyone should go.

It was finally decided that John, Thaddaeus, and James the Just, along with Perpetua, were going to stay in Jerusalem to encourage the people there.

Peter, Matthew, James, and Thomas would flee further into Judea with a few of the other believers.

The rest decided to go their own separate ways.

Philip chose to go to Samaria, to preach to the people who would receive the message.

Finally, after the decisions were made, each group went their different ways.

Hugging her friends goodbye was hard. She never wanted this to happen, but remembering Jesus' words, 'When you are persecuted in one city, flee to the next.' she decided to be brave.

Perpetua thought, as she waved goodbye, *This is going to be challenging, hiding from Saul. But come what may, I'm on this adventure for a lifetime. Keep me strong, dear Lord!*

Chapter 7

Samaria

Since the soldiers were always keeping watch on the building where the believers used to meet, the followers felt it best to meet up in smaller groups, secretly hidden, in certain homes.

Thaddaeus and Perpetua found that, among the gentile merchants, there were people who sincerely cared for them.

These people would keep them alerted on what was taking place and were a tremendous help to the believers when it came time for secret meetings.

A few weeks after the dispersing of the group, Perpetua was, again, walking by the temple.

Going in this time, because she was meeting with someone to pray, she saw Susanna and Nahum being led to the whipping post again.

Susanna looked starved and beaten, Nahum looked pale and worn out. They were struggling to move, and each step was slow and painful.

Feelings of deep sorrow and memories of Stephan came hurtling back into her mind.

Perpetua watched a little longer as officers marched the two up to the whipping post, again. Susanna clung to Nahum. She had almost no strength left.

Following close behind the two, was Saul and Julius. Turning, Perpetua's eyes filled with tears. She couldn't bear to endure this again.

When it had been Stephan, she had tried to convince herself that everything would be alright, and that everything would be happy in the end.

Knowing that happiness was not always the case in these situations, she turned back around and ran to the whipping block, just as the first stripe fell on Susanna.

Throwing herself in front of the guard, Perpetua took the next blow that would have hit Susanna.

The whip's sharp tip found its mark under her left eye.

Wincing, she stood back up to defend the woman, but the guard had already returned to whipping her mercilessly.

Diving over Susanna, Perpetua took three marks to her back.

Julius then stepped in and grabbed the girl. "What's gotten into you, girl?" he asked, angrily.

Perpetua tried to shake free but the twenty-one-year-old was trained well; He was very strong.

She could only watch as one of her closest friends, was whipped again.

Thankfully, as Julius was about to take her into the council, an emergency council meeting was called. The meeting required all who associated with Saul to be there.

Throwing her to the ground, Julius marched into the council room.

Picking herself up and dusting off her scraped elbow, Perpetua ambled over to Susanna.

"Perpetua." The woman's voice was very weak.

"Yes?" the girl said, quite concerned.

"I do not think I can endure another whipping." Susanna said, close to fainting.

"You're not giving up the faith, are you?" Perpetua questioned.

Susanna shook her head, carefully. "No," she said quietly. "I just need a place to rest. Please, help me out of here!" she begged.

Looking over to where Nahum was, Perpetua nodded. "We'll get you somewhere safe. Both of you. Don't worry."

Nahum, who was doing only a little better than his wife, tried to stand to help her.

Perpetua shook her head, "No, no, no, let me help both of you up."

Carefully, she helped Susanna get to her feet. Then she went over and helped Nahum get up.

Slowly, the small group walked through the street. Turning into the house where some of the believers were hidden, Perpetua called into the doorway, "Hello?"

A man appeared in the doorway and smiled. "Perpetua!" he said, cheerfully.

A few minutes later, Nahum and Susanna were laying down in comfortable beds.

Nahum was asleep. Susanna was in pain. Perpetua sat near her to keep her comfortable.

"Perpetua?" the woman called.

The teen looked up from her writing (she was writing a letter to Peter, giving him the details of what had been going on) and smiled. "Yes?" she said quietly.

"I think...I...I think I will not last much longer." The woman stammered.

Perpetua put her letter down and stood up beside the bed. "Are you uncomfortable?" she asked.

Susanna shook her head. "No, I feel no pain." she said slowly.

Perpetua looked over Susanna's battered body. "You think your time is here?" she asked, gently.

Susanna nodded. "I think it's time for me to rest. Will you tell me the story of The Garden?"

Perpetua nodded, the tears now brimming in her eyes. “Eden? Of course.” she whispered.

When Perpetua finished the story, Susanna said, weakly, “Thank you. I know that when I awake, I will behold my Savior.”

Smiling fondly, Susanna sighed. Perpetua took her hand. “His will not, mine.” Perpetua said softly.

Susanna smiled and breathed out. Perpetua looked up to the ceiling.

There were no words of anger this time. She smiled. She knew that her friend was asleep.

Susanna wouldn’t have to worry about seeing Saul again. She wouldn’t have to see anyone in pain ever again.

Perpetua looked at the still figure in the bed. Tears fell gently from her face onto the sheets.

Wiping them away, Perpetua straightened. She knew she would have to be the one to tell the believers about Susanna's death.

Knowing that Mary and Joanna would take it the hardest, she resolved to find a way to quickly get a message to them.

Three days later, the believers lowered a sheet wrapped body into a well dug grave.

Perpetua stood next to Nahum (who only stood a few inches taller than her) to give him comfort during this time.

Nahum, after the funeral, turned to Perpetua. "Thank you!" he said. Perpetua looked surprised. "What for?" she asked.

"You were there with my wife right before she died. I cannot thank you enough for getting us out of the temple just in time," he said.

"She no longer has to suffer." Perpetua said, cheerfully.

After the death of Susanna, the persecution of the followers continued.

Many died. Many more were badly wounded.

Perpetua sometimes wondered why the persecution had to be so bad. She soon discovered that with the worst persecution came the sweet pleasure of knowing that they were found worthy to suffer for Jesus' name.

When the persecution got really bad however, John and Thaddaeus decided they would go and see what progress Philip was having in Samaria.

So, packing a few objects for the trip, John, Thaddaeus, and Perpetua left Jerusalem to go and see what was happening in Samaria.

A few days later, the travelers arrived in Samaria.

"Whew!" Thaddaeus breathed. "That was quite the trip!"

John laughed. "I can agree with you there, brother. Perpetua, how are you faring?"

Perpetua's cheeks were pink from the heat, but she smiled. Calling to the two up ahead she said, "I'm doing well! Are we here?"

John nodded, "Yep, I believe we are. Now, we just have to find Philip."

It didn't take long to find him. There were crowds of people pushing and shoving all around the man.

When Philip spotted them, he dispersed the crowd and greeted his friends. "Good day, brothers and sister," he said warmly.

"Hello!" Thaddaeus greeted. "I can see you've traveled far to make it." Philip said, looking over their dusty, travel worn faces.

John chuckled. "We had to encounter a couple snakes and a wolf, but we're here."

Philip then took them to the place where he was living.

It was quite extravagant. Two stories and a courtyard. It even had a fountain in the front. The people, he said, had been very generous.

It didn't take long before the people wanted to hear from the newcomers. John and Thaddaeus went out to speak to the people, returning in the late evening.

Over a dinner of bread, olives, nuts, and a big pot of lentil soup, the four talked about their travel and the work taking place in Samaria.

Philip had just finished telling a story about healing a deaf man when Thaddaeus asked Perpetua, "What would you think about preaching?"

She got a little shy. "I think it would be interesting." she said, quietly.

John swallowed down some soup and said, "I think it's a wonderful idea!" Philip agreed.

The next day, Perpetua went into town to pick up a couple things at market.

She was taking her time picking out clusters of grapes and the fragrant strawberries, when a woman came up next to her and asked her, “Are you with those men who came to town yesterday?”

Perpetua nodded and smiled. “I am.”

“Are you one of the followers of the man, Jesus of Nazareth?” the woman asked.

Perpetua said, “Yes. I’ve been a believer for about a year. Did you learn from Philip?”

The woman chuckled as she picked up a peach, testing its ripeness. “No, I learned from *Him*.”

Perpetua was now eager to learn more about this woman. The two purchased their items and moved on to another booth.

“You learned from *Jesus*?” Perpetua asked, amazed.

The woman nodded. “Yes. I actually met Him at a well. The well on that hill over there.”

“Isn’t that a bit far away to be getting water from way up there?” Perpetua asked.

The woman laughed heartily. “It is. But, at that time, I was an outcast. I had done many things that I’m not proud of.”

“When I met Him, He told me everything I had ever done. I was so astonished. I then ran into town to get everyone to come and hear Him.”

The two were feeling fabric at the next booth as the woman kept talking.

“He preached to us for three days and at the end, many were believers in His message.”

“That’s how I know Him.” The woman concluded her story. “What about you?” she asked Perpetua.

Perpetua smiled. “It’s a long story.”

The woman chuckled. “Sit here at the fountain and tell me all about it.” she said.

Perpetua sighed. “Where do I start?”

Shaina, the woman, smiled. “Wherever you like.”

“Well, I grew up as the youngest daughter of the tribune, Marcus Antonius. I grew up with wealth and position, but I gave it up for the friendship and love of Jesus Christ.

“I have many friends with the believers, but my closest friend is Jesus. I have suffered much already for Him and I don’t regret it.”

Just then a short man, standing close by asked, “Who is this Jesus that you two speak so much about?”

Perpetua smiled, “Come closer brother, so that I don’t have to shout over the market.” The man smiled and came over and sat down.

Perpetua thought for a moment. *Where should I start?* Then, she said with great enthusiasm,

"Jesus is the Son of God. He came here to teach us the love of His Father. He came to deliver us from the snare of sin so that we can live forever with Him one day in heaven.

"Jesus is willing to forgive those who have sinned. All we have to do is ask. Let me tell you a story.

"There once was a young man who asked his father if he could have his inheritance money. Unlike what most fathers might have done, this father gave his son what he had asked for.

"The son took the money and ran away from home. He went to a big city and wasted his money on frivolous things such as, drinking, parties, and expensive places to stay."

Just then the man broke in saying, "The wretch! He did not deserve the kindness of his father!"

Perpetua smiled and nodded as she continued. “It’s true, he didn’t. But I’m not finished.

“As the boy kept on living his life of drunkenness, he didn’t notice that his money was slowly dwindling away.

“There finally came a point in time, though, when the money ran out. At this same time, a famine had swept through the land and there was no work for anyone.

“The boy searched everywhere trying to find a job, but no one would hire him; at last, however, a man offered him a job feeding his pigs.

“As the weeks passed, the boy grew so hungry that the slops he was feeding the pigs looked good. It was then that he came to his senses and thought,

“My father’s servants are better off than I am right now. I know what I’ll do, I will go back home and beg my father to allow me to be one of his servants. Then, at least, I can have a warm bed and *actual* food!

"So, the boy headed home. Meanwhile, the father, ever since the boy had left, had looked down the road every day to see if the boy was coming.

"I'm sure you can imagine his joy and surprise that day, when he saw the figure of his son coming down the road.

"He ran out to meet the boy and grasped him in his arms. The boy was never able to ask to be servant, because his father called for his servants to make a feast 'For my son that was dead is now alive!' he said.

"And so, my friends," the girl concluded her story, "There is joy in the presence of the angels of God over one sinner that repents."

By the time Perpetua had finished telling the story of The Prodigal Son, a huge crowd had surrounded her. Questions about the Messiah flew back and forth.

Patiently, she answered the questions and showed the people that God desired to have them home with him in heaven, safe and sound.

Three hours later, when the crowd had dispersed, Perpetua walked back to where the three men had been preaching.

Going inside the house, she found John and Thaddaeus, sitting down at the table talking.

“Good evening!” she said happily.

John and Thaddaeus looked up and smiled, apparently relieved.

“Where have you been?” Thaddaeus asked.

Perpetua smiled. “Preaching,” she said.

John and Thaddaeus smiled and nodded to each other.

“Well, it looks like we’ve started a fire here in Samaria.” John said.

Thaddaeus and John stood up and hugged the girl as they prayed, “Keep us strong. For through trial and persecution, you make us perfect.”

Perpetua smiled. *John’s right, we’ve set the world on fire.*

Chapter 8

Surprises in Bethlehem

There was much joy in Samaria. Many had been healed of sickness and still more were freed of demons.

Perpetua, had gotten the opportunity to preach to many of the people there and had brought many new believers to the gospel.

Shaina had been there every step of the way, to encourage and to uplift Perpetua when she needed it.

One day, after being in Samaria for several months, Thaddaeus and John thought it was time to move to another city.

They had been there for enough time, and Jesus had said that they must take the message to the ends of the earth.

Samaria, having been richly blessed by the presence of the apostles, had grown to love the truth and many had become followers.

It was the fourth day of the week when the two, John and Thaddaeus, came into the house to bring Perpetua the news of their decision.

Perpetua was working on sewing a patch onto a little boy's tunic when they came in.

"Hello, you two!" she said warmly.

John smiled. "Good afternoon, Perpetua," he replied. "We've come to a decision; you may want to put that down for a minute," John said, carefully.

Putting down her mending, Perpetua looked up at the two men. "Yes?"

Thaddaeus took a quick shallow breath and dove into what he had to say. "You know that we were told by Jesus that the message of His salvation must go to every nation, tribe, country, people… well you get the idea."

Perpetua chuckled. "After that list, I think so," she said.

Thaddaeus laughed and then continued, "Anyway, John and I think it would be wise, now that Philip has a steady mission work here, to move on," he said, cautiously, waiting for her reaction.

Perpetua took in a deep breath. "Move on where?"

John looked at Thaddaeus and then at the teen. "Bethlehem. The birthplace of our Lord," he said.

When he finished, Perpetua thought she could sense slight excitement in his voice.

"It sounds good to me! When do you want to leave? Although, with the week so advanced wouldn't it be wiser to wait until the new week to begin our travel?"

Thaddaeus chuckled. “With your newest age I believe that you have also obtained maturity.”

It was true. Perpetua, since turning seventeen, had become a very mature girl and had a lot of wisdom for her age.

“You’re right, of course,” John said, “We’ve been thinking about that. As you mentioned, the beginning of the week is the best to leave for a trip. We’re hoping to be leaving the day after Shabbat.”

When the time came for the small group to leave, they gathered with their brothers and sisters to pray.

Philip said the prayer for protection on their journey, protection from Saul, and the blessing of the Holy Spirit on their work in Bethlehem.

After the prayer, the group of three hugged their friends and headed out of the city.

The trip to Bethlehem wasn’t very long, and they arrived in about a day and a half.

On their arrival, they found Mary and Joanna already there. Thaddaeus drew Perpetua's attention to the two women who were sharing food with the hungry.

"Is that Mary?" she asked, excitedly. John nodded. "I thought I would surprise you." he said, smiling.

Running to the women Perpetua said, "Mary! Joanna! It's me!"

Looking up, the two women saw their young friend running towards them.

"Perpetua!" Joanna said, smiling.

When the three ladies grouped up, there was a lot of storytelling and laughing.

When Perpetua told of Susanna, Mary and Joanna looked sad and pained. The feeling didn't last long though, there was too much to get done.

Later that evening, Mary showed the three travelers to their rooms. The rooms were small but cozy. They had a bed and a small oil lamp for light.

As Perpetua slipped into bed that night, she could hear the three, Mary, John, and Thaddaeus, talking quietly at the dining room table.

“What have you heard from Jerusalem?” Mary asked.

“Nothing as of yet.” John replied.

“I got word from James (the Just) that the persecution is as bad as it was when we left. Maybe even worse.” Thaddaeus said, sadly.

“Hmm.” Mary said, thoughtfully. “I feel sorry for all of the believers there.”

The next morning, Perpetua helped Joanna take clothes to some children who needed them and later in the afternoon, Joanna took her to hear Jonathan, a new convert to the faith, share his testimony.

As she listened, another teenager, about a year older than she, came and stood near her.

"Pretty interesting, huh?" he asked in a whisper. Perpetua looked at him and smiled, "Why do ask?"

The boy laughed quietly and said, "He's my father."

Now fully interested in the man's testimony, Perpetua listened intently.

She heard him say that he had abused his wife and three sons. He said that when his wife had finally had enough, she left him.

She wanted to take the boys with her, and all save one left with her.

The man said that shortly after that, a man met with him and told him about Jesus. He immediately confessed his sins and asked forgiveness from his remaining son.

The boy had immediately forgiven him and the two became very close.

At the close of the testimony, Perpetua turned to the boy.

"That was you?" she asked, astonished. He nodded. "Pretty fascinating, isn't it?"

Perpetua nodded vigorously. "Yes it was!"

"I'm Titus," the boy said.

"Perpetua," the girl said.

"Nice to meet you."

In the weeks that followed, Perpetua and Titus became very good friends. They traveled around with Joanna and Mary or John and Thaddaeus helping people where they could.

One day as the two were delivering food and clothes to a few orphans, Titus looked up and said, "Is it completely normal for there to be a man coming into town with soldiers?"

Perpetua looked at where he was now pointing.

When she saw the uniformed soldiers and the appearance of a priest leading them, she said to Titus, “We need to go. Now!”

Nodding, Titus helped her pick up the soup and bowls and showed her the back-route home. Arriving, the two ran in and said, “They’re here. Saul’s here!”

John and Mary looked quickly at each other. “Already?” the woman said quickly.

As she started packing things to go, Mary asked what they had seen. Titus, being the better spokesman, told what they had seen coming through the gates.

Nodding quickly, Mary beckoned for John and Thaddaeus to take a sack for each of them, then looking at Titus, Mary said, “Guide them to Abigail’s house. She has a few underground rooms. You’ll be safe there.”

Soon, the small group consisting of John, Thaddaeus, Perpetua, Jonathan, and Titus, secretly ambled their way through the city where thirty-four years ago the Savior had been born.

Arriving at Abigail's home, Titus knocked rapidly.

A jolly heavyset woman appeared at the door. “Hello?” she said in a thick accent.

Titus' face gave the woman all she needed to know about the situation.

Showing the small group down three flights of stairs, Abigail showed them four rooms where they would be safe. Titus followed her back upstairs promising to return as soon as he could.

Perpetua watched as the hatch door closed and only the light of the torches lit the way up and down the stairs.

A feeling of satisfaction and concern rose inside of her. Going to John and Thaddaeus she shared her concerns.

"I don't fear for myself; I fear that if Saul catches you two, all the work we've done will come to nothing. I know God has a plan through this. What that is, I'm still trying to figure out."

John smiled. "I know you're concerned. Don't worry. We have good friends to help us. Not just earthly ones either," he said gently.

Thaddaeus raised an eyebrow. "You know, Perpetua, I never thought that I would have any adventure in my life. I thought that I would live a boring life with nothing to live up to.

"Now, I know better. Jesus has called us to a work that will take us on many adventures. He not only has promised adventure through danger, but He also promised that He would be with us through it."

Perpetua smiled. "You're right," she said.

The next morning, Titus returned with word from the streets. "Saul is searching everywhere for you all. He has captured Mary and Joanna, but they were released a few hours ago."

John nodded. "I understand that our work here was short lived, but I believe this is God's way of calling us back to Jerusalem."

Thaddaeus agreed. "He's has a point. Though our work here was short, it has been blessed. Maybe God needs us back in Jerusalem. Jesus said, 'When you are persecuted in one city flee to another.'"

Perpetua nodded slowly. Maybe this *was* God's way of getting them back to Jerusalem.

In the days that followed, preparation was being made. The night before they left, Perpetua was helping John pack the food for the trip back to Jerusalem.

While they were packing, Perpetua could hear hurried footsteps coming downstairs.

Abigail burst through the door, breathless. “I…I…I need to…tell you…something!” she said.

“Go on.” John said, slightly concerned. “It’s Saul! He’s coming here!” the woman said.

Quickly picking up the few belongings they had, John, Thaddaeus, and Perpetua quietly went up the stairs and opened the hatch door.

They found the back door and, after thanking Abigail for her hospitality, found Titus, with a donkey drawn cart, ready to go.

Loading all their things into the cart, John moved a few things around and helped the girl up into it.

Getting settled, Perpetua turned toward Titus and hugged him goodbye. He didn’t say anything. He simply moved to the front of the cart to speak with Thaddaeus.

A little while later, he came back and said, “Doesn’t look like ‘Goodbye’ after all.”

Raising an eyebrow, Perpetua said, “What are you talking about?”

Smiling broadly, he grabbed hold of the reins and said, “I’m going with you!”

Chapter 9

Hide and Seek

Perpetua's eyes widened. "What?" she said, shocked.

Titus chuckled as he led the donkey toward the gate of the city. "Surprised?" he asked with a wink.

Perpetua sat back against a bag of food and sighed happily. "A little, I suppose," she said, chuckling. "Did your father let you come?" she asked.

Titus nodded. "He was captured by Saul this morning. Before leaving, he told me to run and ask Abigail if I could go with you all. Needless to say, right after he got taken, I ran to ask. She said yes, so that suited me fine."

Carefully sneaking out of the city, the small group headed out toward the desert, again.

A few hours down the road John started laughing. Thaddaeus, Perpetua, and Titus, looked at him curiously. “Are you alright?” the girl asked, quizzically.

Regaining his composer, he smiled fondly and said, “I was just thinking about the fact that, someone is always running out of Bethlehem. The Savior and now us.”

Nodding understandingly, Thaddaeus said, “Well, I’m glad to see that you’re not suffering from dehydration.”

Titus laughed as he said, “I thought I might have to shove some water down your throat just to get you to calm down! Glad to see I don’t have to!”

The group chuckled and continued their journey. Arriving five hours later, the four had to ditch their cart to get into the city.

It was swarming with people but not very many believers. They slowly made their way to Rachel and Malachi’s home, they had received word a few days prior that they had been released from jail a few months before.

When they made it to the house, they started discussing who should knock.

"You should do it, John," Thaddaeus said.

"No. You should," John said.

"I agree with Thaddaeus on this one," Titus said.

"See? The boy agrees with me. Come on, just knock. It's simple."

"Hey, if it's so simple, why don't you…" John never finished.

Hearing a sudden knocking, the men and boy looked up.

They saw Perpetua standing at the top step, knocking at the door.

They all made different faces. One of confusion, one of humor, and the other of 'I-told-you-so'.

"What?" Perpetua asked. The men just shook their heads and laughed.

The door opened and they were ushered inside. Coming in, after their eyes adjusted to the low light, they saw a simply furnished room and a man sitting at the table.

"It's good to see you!" Rachel said. John nodded and Thaddaeus asked, "Didn't you have six children?"

Rachel nodded. "The oppression became too much for them. They gave up the faith and were taken to other families. We get to see them only from a distance."

Perpetua felt sad for Rachel and Malachi losing their children. She knew, all too well, the pain of losing family.

Even though her family had disowned her shortly after Justina's wedding, Perpetua still considered them *her* family. She prayed that somehow, God would reach her family and bring them back together again.

Wiping away the few tears that had gathered in her eyes, Perpetua straightened and listened to what Rachel had to say.

She said that the persecution in Jerusalem was terrible, but those who were true to the faith stood firm, even to the cost of their lives.

Smiling at this, Rachel then looked at Titus.

"And who is this?" she asked.

Titus smiled and stretched out his hand. "Titus," he said, warmly.

"Where do you come from, Titus? I don't recognize your accent," she asked, now fully curious.

He motioned for a chair as he said, "It's a long story. Shall we take a seat?"

Rachel nodded and sat down. He then went into his story of his father being an abusive father and alcoholic all the way through to him becoming a believer.

"Where does your father come from, Titus?" Rachel asked.

"We came from Antioch and then moved to Bethlehem. Father said there would be better catches for customers there, and he was right. Catches of souls for Jesus. The best customers ever!" Titus said.

A look of utter amazement was printed on the woman's face. "That was beautiful!" she finally said.

"Oh! Would you just look at how late it is! I need to show you to your rooms. Come this way," she said.

Following Rachel to a small closet, the group watched her remove a square piece of wood from the floor.

Once removed, they saw a long staircase leading down underground.

"I'm sure you've seen one of these before," Rachel said. "It's like a whole house under there. We made it just for hiding."

Taking a small lamp, Rachel showed them down and into the living room of the downstairs home.

"Thank you so much, Rachel." Perpetua said, smiling.

Saying goodbye, Rachel went back upstairs. "I'll leave the lamp here with you," she said, "There are torches for light down here. Stay safe."

After getting settled into their separate rooms, the four met back in the living room to sit and talk.

It was a nicely sized room with four couches. They each took one and began discussing their plan of action.

"We know that Saul will probably be back as soon as he discovers we're not in Bethlehem anymore. So, we should plan to reach as many people as quickly as we can." John said.

Nodding in agreement, Thaddaeus said, "We should have a way to alert each other when we're preaching. We know that Saul's not the only one we need to watch out for. The priests and the Romans are going to be on the lookout for us too."

With her hand resting on her chin in thought, Perpetua said, "What if we had time that we would set aside every day for teaching? We could switch where we meet too, just so that we keep the leaders on their toes."

Titus nodded. "She has a good point," he said. "Kind of like a mixed game of tag and hide-and-seek."

The men nodded. "I like it," John said.

A few weeks passed since their arrival in Jerusalem and soon the hiding became a challenge.

There came a time when Perpetua and Titus were helping some of the believers move out of their homes. They had become so exasperated by the persecution in Jerusalem that they had made up their minds to go somewhere else.

Titus had tried to encourage them to stay, but they were thoroughly convinced that they needed to leave.

As she packed the last few things in the cart, Perpetua turned to Hadassah and said, “We will miss you.” Hadassah smiled and said, “Thank you. I will miss you as well.”

Titus helped the young children into the cart and double checked everything’s security.

When at last all was ready, the family drove away leaving Titus and Perpetua waving.

“Do you think we will ever see them again?” Titus asked solemnly. Perpetua shrugged as they turned toward home.

Several months later, when Titus and Perpetua were looking for a place to hold a meeting, Perpetua saw a roman woman following them.

Drawing Titus’s attention to the lady, Perpetua said, “She reminds me so much of Matertera Maia.”

Titus nodded. “I understand how you feel. What do you propose we do?”

“Hmm.” Perpetua said. “The last time I encountered any of my family members, I sincerely regretted it.”

Titus shrugged his shoulders. “It’s up to you,” he said after a little while.

“Perpetua!” the woman called.

Shocked, Perpetua stopped. She didn’t want to talk to Matertera Maia.

Since becoming a Christian, there had been very few *good* meetings with her family.

Maia started walking toward her, a quizzical look on her face. Perpetua did not wish to bring more harm upon herself than she already had.

Looking quickly at Titus she asked, “What should we do?” Titus watched the woman coming toward them.

Observing the situation at hand, he motioned for her to follow him down the street.

As they walked quickly down the street, Perpetua could hear Matertera Maia picking up her pace behind them.

"Titus, she's following us," Perpetua said. Titus nodded and took a left, down an alleyway to try and lose their pursuer.

They came out of the alley onto a street that was a few streets from Rachel's house.

Not seeing Matertera Maia, they sighed with relief and the two began winding their way home.

Just as the two were rounding a corner, Titus said, "I hate to be the bearer of bad news but, there's a group coming very quickly into town.

Perpetua looked up. "Oh dear," she said.

The group was easily recognizable by its leader: Saul of Tarsus.

"Well," Titus said, "looks like another game of hide-and-seek here in Jerusalem."

Just as the two were about to enter the house, Perpetua heard a noise. Down the road she saw Matertera Maia coming down the street on a horse.

"Oh no!" Perpetua said.

Running in to the house, Titus said to Rachel, "If there's a knock on the door, know that it's danger."

Nodding, she ushered the two to the closet. Giving them a lamp, she waved 'Goodbye'.

Just as the hatch closed over their heads, Titus and Perpetua heard knocking at the door.

Chapter 10

A Home for Augustus

Hurrying down the steps toward their rooms, Titus and Perpetua stopped just far away from the hatch so that, if it were opened, they wouldn't be seen, but they could hear everything that was going on.

Titus smiled while breathing heavily, trying to catch his breath. "Talk about a game of hide-and-seek!" he said, chuckling lightly.

Perpetua's focus was listening to what was going on at the front door. She was waiting for the moment it would open, and her aunt would enter, trying to find both her and Titus.

She could hear some talking between Rachel and Malachi, but not much else. In a tense whisper she asked Titus, "Do you think she's coming?"

He shrugged and said, “We heard the knock. Maybe Rachel’s afraid of romans.”

Perpetua glared at him and then looked back up at the hatch. There was no noise.

Stifling a laugh, Titus motioned for her to follow him further downstairs. “What are we going to do?” she asked in a whisper.

Titus said nothing but kept going downstairs until they got to their home underground.

John greeted them. “Did you find a place?” he asked. Perpetua nodded and said, “We did. We also picked up a tracker as well.”

Nodding understandably, John turned to Thaddaeus who was busy fixing a broken cartwheel.

“Well,” John began, “It looks like this game of hide-and-seek is increasing its players!” he said to Thaddaeus.

Thaddaeus looked at the two teens. “Who followed you?” he asked. Perpetua was going to answer when, they heard the hatch open.

Looking at John, she asked in a whisper, “What do you want to do?”

John motioned for everyone to go to their rooms and remain quiet. He and Thaddaeus said that they would stay in the living room.

When Perpetua entered her room, she immediately went to her bed and knelt down.

Praying with all her heart she said, “Lord, you promised that you would be with us to the end of the world! You promised that you would give us courage when we were enduring trial. Keep us, your followers, in perfect peace, I trust you Father!”

Perpetua got up and sat down on her bed. She listened to the noises coming from the living room (which weren’t very many).

She heard John talking with someone and she heard Thaddaeus explaining why he was fixing a cartwheel.

She then heard Rachel say, “There was a lady who came in, she looked roman. She said that she had seen her niece run into our house. I don’t what she’s talking about.”

Perpetua chuckled lightly. Matertera Maia was definitely looking for her, that was obvious. What wasn’t so obvious was why.

Perpetua wondered why her family wanted to know her whereabouts. After Justina’s wedding, they had made it a point to never see her.

Confused and troubled, she waited until John knocked on her door before she came out. John looked relieved.

“Who was it?” Perpetua asked. John shook his head, “I have no idea. Rachel was saying that there was a roman lady upstairs who was asking about her niece.”

Perpetua sighed and said, “It was probably one of my Materteras. What I still don’t understand, though, is why?”

John shook his head, “I’m sure God will reveal that in His own good way, in His own good time. Anyway, we should get ready to go out and preach.”

Shortly after getting ready, the group of four, John, Thaddaeus, Titus, and Perpetua, headed out to a place where they would be teaching the people.

Arriving, they saw that a group had gathered around James (the Just). “Perfect!” John said, smiling broadly.

Titus and Perpetua took their posts right outside of the group of listeners.

“Am I the only one who enjoys this work so much?” Titus asked. Perpetua shook her head. “No. I enjoy every last minute of it too.”

Looking out into the streets, Perpetua could see people chasing something their direction.

"Hey, Titus, can you see that group coming straight for us?" Perpetua asked.

Looking up from his wood carving, Titus saw the same thing that she did. "Uh…yeah, I see it. Should we alert the group?"

Perpetua took in the situation carefully. "Not yet. If they keep coming straight for us, then yes."

Several minutes later, the group was still running toward the group of believers.

"Titus, alert James (the Just) that we have trouble." Perpetua said.

Nodding, Titus grabbed the long piece of red cloth that they used to alert each other of danger and waved it so that James could see it.

Catching sight of the cloth, James said to those gathered, "Dear ones, we must disperse. I will continue my sermon the next time we meet."

The group quickly split up and went for safe places. John, Thaddaeus, James, Titus, and Perpetua went for their home.

James didn't live with them, but he liked to walk with them to make sure they arrived safely where they went.

As they were nearing Rachel and Malachi's house, James said, "Does anyone know what kind of trouble was headed our direction?"

Titus smiled and chuckled. "Well, in my imagination it was some kind of horrible evil." he said, raising an eyebrow in Perpetua's direction.

Perpetua laughed and rolled her eyes playfully. "Ahh!" James said.

When the group made it to Rachel and Malachi's home, they waved goodbye to James and went inside.

"Oh! Praise God you all made back safely!" Rachel said, obviously relived.

“What happened?” Thaddaeus asked.

“It’s Saul. He captured Tehilim and Iyov and tried to find out where *you* were!” Rachel said, “I’m just glad to see he didn’t find you.”

In the underground living room, the four, John, Thaddaeus, Titus, and Perpetua, were discussing the situation they were now dealing with.

John mentioned that, now that they were back in Jerusalem, Perpetua’s family would probably try, more than ever before, to bring Perpetua back home.

Titus said that even though there was this new danger, they shouldn’t lighten up on the ministry just to keep themselves safe.

Thaddaeus agreed with Titus and added that they should probably pick up the work even more now that there was more danger.

Nodding, Perpetua said, “I completely agree with all of that.

However, we should probably consider the fact that my father is a tribune. Having that high-ranking position, he can take me into court and eventually send me to my death.

"Now, I am not saying that I'm afraid of dying, I am only saying that we should be extra cautious."

"I also understand that we've been here in Jerusalem a while, so if this is a sign from God saying to move on, I will accept it."

Titus nodded. "She does have a good point. Let's take this to the Lord in prayer."

So, the small group knelt down and began to pray. They hadn't gotten very far when Rachel came running downstairs.

"Sorry to interrupt you, but there's a woman here to see you." Rachel said, pointing at Perpetua.

Raising an eyebrow, Perpetua asked, "Did she call me specifically?" Rachel nodded emphatically.

Perpetua frowned and looked at the others. They nodded encouragingly at her. So, she stood up and followed the older woman upstairs.

Once upstairs, Perpetua saw her Matertera Maia. "Matertera," Perpetua said.

"Darling," Maia said, quietly. "I have been following you trying to get your attention for a little while now."

Perpetua pressed her lips together to keep from laughing. Matertera Maia continued, "I know I'm not supposed to see you, but there's something I need to ask of you."

Perpetua looked slightly confused. Since the separation from her family, she wasn't allowed to have favors asked of her, or so she thought.

Maia went on, "Since your mother gave me guardianship over you three children when she died, I have guardianship over Augustus. I know that you, being eighteen, and Justina being twenty-one, are now independent, so this won't affect you.

"I want to give Augustus to you. Now that your old enough to have this responsibility I would like you to take it," she said.

Perpetua's eyes got wide. "So, you're asking me to take guardianship of Gus?" she asked, skeptically.

Maia nodded. "Yes. He needs stability. He has been moved around from Justina's house, back to his father's, and then to me and Matertera Fortuna."

Perpetua looked at her feet. "I'm glad that you think me responsible enough to take my own brother, but I cannot.

Looking into her aunt's eyes, Perpetua asked, "Since you're so concerned with finding Augustus a home, why don't you keep him?"

Maia's face grew stern. "I'm getting older, Perpetua. I need my time to myself. You are young, and you, as his older sister, should be able to find time to care for him."

Perpetua took in a deep breath and said, "I travel around Judea a lot and to accept Augustus would be to put him mortal danger.

"Not just that, you must remember that I am no longer part of the Antonius family."

Matertera Maia nodded slowly, "I forgot about that. I understand."

"I would love to have him, but I already put my own life in peril so often, that to even think of putting one of my family members in the same predicament as I, would cause me much grief," Perpetua said, watching her aunt's reaction carefully.

Matertera Maia smiled. "I'm glad to see that you have matured enough to start thinking of others. I will, however, have to continue looking for a new place for the poor boy."

Perpetua folded her arms and rested her hand on her upper lip. "If you want your time to yourself, and you want someone to take the responsibility of having Gus, I think I may know someone," she said thoughtfully.

Matertera Maia cocked her head. "Who?" she asked in a cool tone.

Perpetua said, "Well, the owner of this house has lost all of her children to the government."

Maia looked confused. "What are you getting at?" she asked, eyebrows raised.

Perpetua shrugged as she said, "Well…you could give Augustus to her…" motioning toward Rachel.

Matertera Maia looked like she might explode. "Do you think I would just leave my nephew in the hands of some Jew?"

Perpetua sighed. "*You* don't want to take the responsibility for him, so in answer to your question, yes."

The middle age woman looked horrified. "Next time, remind me not to ask you for help," she said, straining to remain somewhat calm.

"It was a mistake to come here in the first place!" Matertera Maia said, as she stormed out of the house.

Perpetua shook her head as she turned back toward the closet. Turning to Rachel, she said, "I guess I unveiled my aunt's true feelings. She never did take the time for me or Justina when we were young, and I shouldn't have expected anything different for Gus."

Rachel sighed, "We shouldn't expect any kind of good from unbelievers." Perpetua nodded sadly and lifted the hatch to go to the underground house.

When she arrived downstairs, Titus and John were the only ones still in the living room. John saw the dejected look on her face as she took a seat.

"Are you ok?" he asked quietly.

Perpetua nodded as she wiped away some tears. "I just feel like every time I try to do something helpful, it ends up failing miserably."

Titus stood up and hugged Perpetua. John came and hugged her too.

John said, "That's exactly how we felt when we could cast the demon out of that poor man's son. Helpless."

Perpetua sniffled and said, "I'm glad to know I'm not the only one who has felt this way."

Titus chuckled lightly as he said, "We have to remember that Jesus has felt the way we all do at one time or another."

Wiping her tears away, Perpetua said, "Thank you, Titus. That really helped."

Titus smiled and winked at her. Perpetua laughed and then turned to Thaddaeus who had just walked in.

"Is everything alright in here?" he asked. Perpetua and Titus nodded simultaneously.

Shaking his head and laughing, Thaddaeus went and sat down next to John.

"What's the plan?" he asked, looking over a map that John had of Judea.

John looked over at the map and said, "We've had many people captured recently, as you all know. I think it would be wise if we went somewhere safer."

"Somewhere like where?" Titus asked.

Right before answering, Thaddaeus and John both looked up toward the hatch.

A loud knocking on the front door made the other two look up as well.

“Hide-and-seek?” Titus asked.

John nodded. “Probably.”

“Uh oh.”

Chapter 11

On the Run Again

"Where are we going again?" Perpetua asked in a whisper.

John and Thaddaeus looked at each other. Looking back at Perpetua, Thaddaeus said, "Damascus."

Quickly, both Titus and Perpetua packed their few belongings. Once finished, they met back in the living room. John and Thaddaeus were ready as well.

Quietly, the four walked upstairs. It seemed that every step each person took was loud enough to make the snow fall off of Mount Hermon.

When they made it to the first bend that would lead them up to the hatch, they stopped and listened.

The person coming out of the hatch would see, standing right outside of the closet, to the right, the dining room and kitchen where the day's happenings would take place.

To the left was a hallway leading to the two bedrooms and a back door.

Waiting anxiously, the four people seemed frozen. Upstairs they could hear someone talking with Malachi.

"Rumor has it that you're hiding, not only believers of the dead Messiah, but also a roman," a man said.

Malachi said, "I am not hiding anyone who believes in a *dead* Messiah."

The man stiffened. "Are you trying to lie to me?" he asked. "You know I can take you into custody for this and being a Jew, you know better than to bear false witness," he said, very firmly.

Malachi, boldly said, "I am not hiding anyone who believes in a *dead* Messiah."

The man's face grew red with anger as he stalked out of the house. The door closed behind him in a way that would let the four downstairs know that all was safe.

Coming up, John stayed with Malachi and Rachel to comfort them, while the other three loaded the donkey and got ready for the trip.

Soon, Titus came inside and said, "Alright. We're ready."

After each person hugged Rachel and Malachi, and after Perpetua promised to write to them once a week, they got in the cart and rolled gently away.

How could the two teenagers know that this would be the last time they would ever see these people, Rachel and Malachi? They couldn't.

The trip to Damascus only took a week, but the group ran out of water on the third day, making the trip feel even longer, and the ever-present smelly donkey wasn't helping.

In the cart, Titus sat up groggily. "Hey look! An oasis! Let's go!" he shouted, as much as he could.

John held him down as they kept going. "Hey! Why'd you do that? There was water right there!" Titus said.

Thaddaeus chuckled as he told Titus, "What you see my dear boy is a mirage. If you were to chase your so called 'oasis', you would run yourself into the hot desert never to return."

Titus folded his arms and said, mock-sadly, "Well, I saw water; maybe even a couple of date palms."

Perpetua fumbled around in one of the bags and pulled out a small bottle. "I've been saving this for one of you guys." she said chuckling, "Here Titus, you can have it."

Thanking her, Titus took the bottle and guzzled it. He then looked out to where he thought he had seen the oasis.

“You guys are crazy to ever think of chasing an imaginary oasis!” Titus said jokingly. Perpetua shook her head and settled back into the cart.

When the group finally arrived in Damascus, they met with one of the families of believers and got settled in. There was no underground house here, but it was nice none the less.

Titus downed ten cups of water before he could talk straight, but when he could, he was as jolly and lighthearted as ever.

When the group had finished preaching for the night, they went back home and started getting ready for bed.

“Perpetua?” Titus asked.

Looking up from her meal of bread dipped in oil, and juice, she said, “Yes?”

Titus looked concerned. “I’m worried about the believers here. They are so insecure, and they need help. With Saul running around capturing people, they’re going to need support.”

Perpetua nodded. “I agree. You have a soft heart, Titus. I’m glad to see that you’re back in your right mind.”

Titus laughed and headed to his room. Perpetua sighed. It felt good to be doing such a great work for God.

When the next day came, Titus, Perpetua, and John, headed out to the city.

They ambled through the streets and went looking for a place to start speaking.

As they walked, John asked Titus, “What do you think of preaching, Titus?”

Titus smiled and said, “I think it would be interesting.”

Perpetua laughed. “Titus, you would be terrific at preaching. Your testimony is powerful, and God has blessed your efforts with the children!”

Titus smiled and said, “Maybe. We’ll see. Whatever God wills.”

When they arrived at the meeting place, Titus and Perpetua took their posts right outside the group.

John stood up and began to speak about Jesus and the sermon lasted about two hours.

Once it was over, the four returned to their residence. John and Thaddaeus sat down at the table and began to talk.

"John, I've been burdened with the feeling that we need to return to Samaria. I know we just arrived here in Damascus and we need to strengthen the group; I just feel that something is going to happen in Samaria, and we should be there."

John nodded, and said, "I completely agree."

For the next few weeks, John and Thaddaeus preached and encouraged the people to stay strong in the faith of Jesus Christ. They even started preaching in the synagogue.

The priests in Damascus started complaining to the chief priests in Jerusalem about the believers and the council started plotting against them.

The council was still trying to deal with the believers that were still in Jerusalem when they got the complaints.

Calling a meeting, the council decided to authorize Saul to go to Damascus and arrest the believers there.

Giving him a cohort of soldiers, led by Julius Marci, the council told Saul to leave as soon as possible to be able to catch the believers.

Back in Damascus, John was at the house with a letter in his hand as he was pacing.

The news from the letter was good, but it was making John think.

The teens walked in from outside, laughing as they carried an empty pot of soup.

“You should have seen her face when I told her I wouldn’t accept her money. It was priceless. She tried to force her money on me, but I snuck it back into her purse when she wasn’t looking! It was funny!” Titus said, still laughing.

Perpetua was laughing too. When she caught sight of John, though, she silenced Titus.

“Is something the matter?” she asked John.

John shook his head. “No. I got a letter from Peter today. He wants to go with me to Samaria so we can help Philip.”

Perpetua put the pot down and sat at the table. “When are you planning on leaving? she asked.

John stopped pacing and said, “I’m planning on leaving in three days.”

Titus asked, “What’s going to happen to us?”

John looked from Titus to Perpetua and said, “You two get to choose. Thaddaeus and I will be going, but it’s up to you what you want to do.”

Perpetua looked at Titus and said, “We should pray about this decision.” Nodding, Titus stood up and went to his room.

The next few days were busy ones for Perpetua and Titus. They prayed many times a day for God’s guidance in this big decision.

When the third day came, Perpetua and Titus helped John and Thaddaeus into a cart that they were taking to Samaria.

They had made the decision to stay in Damascus and help the small group of believers there.

As the two teenagers hugged their traveling partners goodbye, they had a strange feeling.

They wouldn't know it, but they would never see John and Thaddaeus, or any of the apostles for that matter, again.

After the two men left, Titus and Perpetua focused more than ever on their work. They were the ones who had to preach now, and they did, with the power of the Holy Spirit.

It had been a few months since John and Thaddaeus had left. Titus would look for word from the two every day and one day a letter came. It stated:

'My dear young friends,

We have missed your company very much and we continue to pray for the work going on there.

We have met up with Peter and Philip and have begun preaching the word here in Samaria again.

While we were preaching the message a few weeks ago, there was a man who had a great amount of control on the people. His name was Simon.

He was a sorcerer and he followed us around for many days. One day, when we were baptizing people in the name of Jesus, he came up to us and asked to be baptized, which we gladly did.

It was a few days after this that he kept following us around, watching us pray for the Holy Spirit to come into different people, when he came up and asked for us to give him the Holy Spirit.

We explained that we could not give him anything that didn't belong to us. We told him that he must be humble and let God change his heart.

At this, he produced a large sum of money and begged for us to give him the Holy Spirit, at which Peter said, "Let your money die with you, because you thought you could purchase the Spirit of the Lord! Confess and repent because of this sin which you have done!"

After that, he went away, and we haven't seen him since.

So dear ones, I must close my letter and say farewell. I miss you both dearly and I pray for you both every day. May God continue to bless your efforts in Damascus and may He protect you in this time of danger.

Your brother in Christ, John'

Running quickly into the house, Titus shouted, "Perpetua! News!"

Coming out of her room, Perpetua saw the letter. "May I?" she asked excitedly.

Handing her the letter, Titus let her read it.

"Oh! This is *so* exciting!" Perpetua said, obviously happy.

Michal (the wife of the man they were staying with) came in from grinding wheat and saw the two completely absorbed in the letter.

"Something good?" she asked.

Titus looked up from the letter and said smiling, “It’s the first word we’ve gotten from John since they left.”

“Oh, I see.” she said, smiling broadly.

It was a few weeks after this event, that the council ordered Julius, without the accompaniment of Saul, to go to Damascus and retrieve his sister-in-law.

This he set out to do immediately. He left Jerusalem with a legion of soldiers under his command (why he went with so many to pick up a small teenage girl, no one really understood).

He left on the second day of the week and traveled for seven days.

In Damascus, Titus and Perpetua were doing the work as best they could. They were being rewarded with many souls who turned to the Lord Jesus Christ.

It was on a sultry afternoon when, Titus, as so often was the case, looked up from the booth he was purchasing goods from and said to Perpetua, "Is it just me, or are there *a lot* of roman soldiers marching into town?"

Looking toward the gate, Perpetua saw the face of her sister's husband.

"Oh dear. It's Julius!" she said, alarmed.

Titus finished buying the goods he had come for and led Perpetua the back route to the house.

"Michal!" Titus called when they made it to the house.

Entering the room, Michal said, "Yes?"

Perpetua went over to her room and started packing her things. As she did so, she told Michal, "There are romans here to take me. I need to escape while I still can."

Michal looked concerned. "Now?" she asked.

Nodding, Perpetua grabbed her small sack and waited for Titus. Titus packed quickly and was soon ready to go.

"Where will you go?" Michal asked anxiously.

Titus picked up his things and began heading for the door. "We'll probably go to Sebastiya. It's closer than anywhere else."

Nodding quickly, Michal handed Perpetua a small pouch of money. "For your trip."

The two hugged Michal and her husband Elkanah and hurried out the back door.

As they ran out the door, they came face to face with Julius Marci.

"Aha! I've caught you at last!" Julius said, triumphantly.

Perpetua straightened. She looked very small compared to Julius, but the boldness inside of her seemed much larger.

"Do you know how long I've been looking for you?" he practically shouted.

Titus stepped forward and pushed Perpetua behind him.

"Is there something we can do for you, officer?" Titus asked very politely.

Julius stepped forward until he was standing right in front of Titus, who only stood a small height of five feet six inches.

"Are you standing up for *my* sister-in-law?" he asked through clenched teeth.

Titus squared his shoulders. "I am," he said calmly.

Julius grabbed Titus' arm as he yelled, "She is *my* property! She belongs in a *roman* family!"

Even though he was getting yelled at in his face, Titus remained calm.

Perpetua grabbed Julius' arm and said, "Let him go! It's me you want."

Julius dropped Titus and grabbed both of Perpetua's arms. "I know it's you I want! I also know that this boy is part of the group that worships the dead Messiah! He's an outlaw!" Julius screamed.

Perpetua kept her focus on his eyes. "Take me where you will. My God is stronger than anything you can do to me. Do what you want, my God, if it's His will, *will* deliver me."

Julius grabbed both teenagers and tied their hands. "Let's see if your God can deliver you from the iron teeth of the great city of Rome!"

Chapter 12

The Patience of the Saints

Tied and gagged, Titus and Perpetua could do nothing to save themselves.

Julius led them to where he and the other soldiers were staying, and quickly began packing his things to return to Jerusalem, and eventually Rome.

The teenagers sat, tied to two chairs at a table, praying with all that was in them for God's protection and His will.

Titus glanced over at Perpetua, now a beautiful girl of nineteen, and realized how much she meant to him.

Tears formed in his eyes at the thought of losing her, but more importantly he was grieved with the thought of losing such a powerful worker for the body of believers.

Perpetua looked at Titus, whose eyes were now clamped shut in prayer, and thought of when she had first met him.

She felt great sorrow, not for herself, but for the friend that would have to endure so much for the sake of the God they both loved so much.

It took Julius a couple of hours before he was ready, but when he was, there was to be no delay.

Untying the two young people, a group of soldiers led them out to a wagon to be transported to Jerusalem.

When at last all was ready, Julius gave the signal and they moved out of Damascus.

Perpetua gazed at the town which had been her home for the last eight months and felt deep sorrow that she had to leave them at this time.

She prayed fervently that God would raise another to take their place and stand as a bold worker for Him.

After arriving back in Jerusalem a week later, Titus and Perpetua were thrown into a jail cell to await news from the capitol as to what should be done with them.

Since they were not Jewish, the two of them had to be judged by roman law, which in that case meant going to Rome to sort everything out.

In Jerusalem, since there was nothing that could be done for them, Julius found a roman ship that would take them to Rome.

It had been a long time since Titus or Perpetua had been on a boat and they soon became seasick. After twenty-eight days on the sea, the group arrived in Rome.

It was a busy city, and they had a hard time getting through all the people. But, eventually, they made it to the prison.

After getting put into another cell, Titus and Perpetua finally had time to talk.

"My dear friend!" Titus said, as soon as the soldiers left.

Perpetua looked up and smiled sadly. "Titus, what are we going to do?"

Titus took her hands in his and said, "We will do what we always do in times of peril; pray."

So, the two knelt down and poured their hearts out to God. They prayed that God would give them wisdom and courage to be able to stand this trial.

Three days after their arrival in Rome, Julius brought a case before the roman governor concerning the two he had captured.

Being an excellent spokesman, he brought his case forward strongly and the governor ruled the case in Julius' favor.

It had been a little over a month since Titus and Perpetua had left Jerusalem and they missed it terribly.

One afternoon, as the two were finishing praying together, four guards came down and said, “The governor has decided against you. You both are to be sent to the Colosseum prison immediately.”

Titus and Perpetua exchanged glances and then stood up to go.

The march to the Colosseum didn’t take very long. When they arrived, the two were filed into a cell and the door locked behind them.

“What is going to become of us, Perpetua?” Titus asked.

Perpetua shook her head. She had a very distant look in her eyes and Titus could tell that she was pondering something weighty.

“Are you alright?” he asked gently.

Perpetua nodded her head and then fell to her knees in tears.

Titus caught her and prayed for her until she calmed down. When she finally did, she spoke, heart breaking with sadness, "Titus, I have a feeling that we are not going to be leaving this prison until the Lord sees fit to lay us to rest. My heart is burdened with sorrow for my family! They have no one to lead them to the precious love of Jesus.

"Maybe, it is God's will that through our death many will be brought to the light of His truth." Titus eventually said.

A week and a half after this incident, a few guests came to visit the two. They were, Marcus Antonius, Matertera Maia, and Jonathan, Titus' father.

There were hugs and tears all around and Marcus turned to his daughter.

"Look at you! You are a woman in all definitions of the word! God has turned you into the most beautiful woman of his creation!" he said, bubbling over with happiness.

"Father!" Perpetua said, "You speak of God as the Creator, do you believe?" she asked, cautiously.

Nodding, Marcus said, "I have been a believer, secretly of course, for about a year."

Hugging her father tightly, Perpetua cried tears of relief.

Shaking her head, she finally spoke, "Father, Titus and my execution is scheduled. There is nothing that can be done."

Marcus lifted her chin and gently tucked a strand of hair behind her ear, and said, "I know. That's why I'm here. To join you in your profession of faith."

Tears filled Perpetua's eyes. "You're here to join me?" she asked.

Smiling, Marcus nodded.

Jonathan and Titus wrapped up their conversation and turned toward Marcus and Perpetua. Smiling broadly, the adults gave Titus and Perpetua some food; the first food they'd had in five days.

Kneeling down, they all prayed for God's protection for Jonathan and Maia as they travelled back home, then they prayed for God's blessing on the simple food that would provide strength and nourishment for the young people.

Marcus had decided to stay and cast his lot with the two young teens. In the time between his arrival and the execution, he told Perpetua about how he came to know Christ and what ended up happening to Augustus.

The now seven-year-old boy had come to know and love Jesus just as his father did. He had been given to Rachel and Malachi after all, and they had been such a blessing to Augustus.

While in prison, Marcus told of how he discovered the love of Christ. It was like this:

After Perpetua had left home for the last time, Marcus had gone in to see the council and he had been a witness to one of the interrogations of one of the believers.

After watching the way they calmly presented their case and how furious the council would get at their message, Marcus decided that he needed to know more.

Finding one of the roman soldiers who had been converted, Marcus asked how he too could become a follower.

He was then introduced to James the Just who led him to a perfect understanding of Jesus and His love. Soon after this, Marcus was baptized in secret and became enthusiastic about sharing Christ.

Because of this, he was deposed from Tribune and told not to show his face in any governmental meeting again, but this suited Marcus just fine.

He started telling more people about the fact that he had been there when Jesus was crucified and he had heard the centurion say, "Surely this Man was the Son of God."

After hearing this from her father, Perpetua threw her arms around him and said, "Father, may God keep you true to Himself now more than ever.

A few weeks after Maia and Jonathan had left, the roman officer came in and ushered Perpetua to another room.

There she saw Justina with a baby girl who sleeping soundly, wrapped up tightly in soft fabric.

"*Soror*!" Justina cried out, stepping forward and hugging her little sister.

"Justina!" Perpetua gasped. "What are you doing here?"

Justina cried into Perpetua's shoulder and said, "I cannot do what Father is doing, but I came to show you your new niece."

Looking down at the baby, Perpetua watched her little eyes flutter open. Her eyes were dark blue, just like Justina's.

Looking up at her sister Perpetua asked, "What's her name?" Justina smiled and, with tears in her eyes said, "I have named her Perpetua, after her brave and steadfast aunt that she will never know or remember."

Perpetua's eyes filled with tears. "Thank you, *Soror*! Thank you!" she said.

It was a week after this, that the scheduled day of execution arrived.

The group of three, Perpetua, Titus, and Marcus, were marched out to the arena to face their fate.

God was merciful even in this place. With thousands of people gathered around to watch the spectacle, God placed his loving hand on Marcus. He faced the line of gladiators.

Kneeling in the soft sand, Marcus lifted his head and said, “Father, into your hands, I commit my spirit.”

As he finished speaking, he was cut down by a blow from a sword to his neck. He died instantly.

Perpetua watched as this man who had become so close to her in just a short time, repeated the words of the Nazarene and laid down his life for Him as well.

As the afternoon drew on, Titus and Perpetua suffered many wounds.

Titus suffered several attacks from a wild boar and a mad bull. When finally, the crowd had enough of watching Titus face the animals, they called for a gladiator to execute him by sword.

Titus stood firm, facing the warrior. The gladiator took his sword and swiftly slashed Titus’ ribs.

Titus fell over in a pool of his own blood and his vision began to fade. Calling for Perpetua, he said to her,

"I lay down my life with the joy and honor of dying for our Lord."

He looked into her deep brown eyes and tucked a strand of stray hair behind her ear.

"Titus," Perpetua said softly, "I know the Lord has already worked a great miracle. He gave me you until I could have my father back. I know that now."

Kneeling over her best friend, she kissed his cheek, now pale with death, and whispered, "Lord, I need you now."

Standing up, Perpetua looked straight into the eyes of Julius Marci and said, "Lord, do not hold this sin against them!"

The gate to an animal cage opened. Turning her head toward it, Perpetua saw a huge male lion.

Turning to face the lion, she had a sudden thought.

I have been fighting against you, the lion who seeks whom he may devour, but I have also had a lion who has stood by my side through the worst of times. He is the Lion of the Tribe of Judah. He will never leave me, and he will never forsake me.

As she thought this, she saw the lion roar and take a step toward her. Closing her eyes, she prayed, 'Lord Jesus, receive my spirit.'

A second later, Perpetua Antonia lay in a mangled mess of her own blood and the crowd cheered.

Justina who had been in the crowd, watching, felt as if a piece of her had died too. She watched as Julius shook his head and buried his face in his cape.

Thomas and Matthew were in Rome at the time and they went, later that day, and retrieved the bodies of the three individuals. They took each body and dug a neat grave for each one.

It was three weeks later that they arrived back in Jerusalem and told the believers what had happened.

The apostles were brokenhearted. They had lost their friend and fellow believer and now they must continue the work that Perpetua could no longer do.

Mary, John and Thaddaeus were distraught and delivering the news to the other believers was very hard for the three people who knew her best.

The believers praised God for such a powerful influence that the young girl had had.

When the time came for the memorial of the three, it was Mary and Thaddaeus who put everything together. The ceremony was beautiful. Flowers lined and decorated everything, and Andrew gave the message of hope.

To all who knew her, Perpetua was a pillar of truth and love. God used her in many ways to reach those who could not be reached.

God's love still shines in His true followers now. When the Unquenchable Fire, the Holy Spirit, has finished his work, Jesus will come, and those who love and loved Him, will go with Him to heaven where they will live forever with the one who lived and died for them.

To Be Continued...

Epilogue

After Perpetua's death, the Christian church expanded all over the world. They never stopped being persecuted, but God kept them faithful in adversity.

James, brother of John, was the first of the apostles to be killed. He was beheaded in Jerusalem, under the orders of King Herod Agrippa I.

The rest of the apostles eventually died too, but not after finishing their work on this earth, by spreading the Unquenchable Fire all over the world.

Saul, the great persecutor of the believers, became converted by Jesus Himself, on the road to Damascus. He would go on to change his name to Paul and become one of the greatest Christian missionaries ever known.

In his own words Paul said,

But I do not want you to be ignorant, brethren, concerning those who have fallen asleep, lest you sorrow as others who have no hope. For if we believe that Jesus died and rose again, even so God will bring with Him those who sleep in Jesus. For this we say to you by the word of the Lord, that we who are alive and remain until the coming of the Lord will by no means precede those who are asleep. For the Lord Himself will descend from heaven with a shout, with the voice of an archangel, and with the trumpet of God. And the dead in Christ will rise first. Then we who are alive and remain shall be caught up together with them in the clouds to meet the Lord in the air. And thus we shall always be with the Lord. Therefore comfort one another with these words.

1 Thessalonians 4:13-18

Paul knew that the believers would not need to worry about their loved ones who had died. Jesus would soon come again and all who trusted in Him would go to heaven with Him.

The love of Jesus has changed many hearts and will continue to do so. Jesus will not come until His followers have taken His message to all the world.

Like the believers of old, God is raising up a people who will use the gift of the Holy Spirit to preach His good news everywhere.

We each have the decision to choose whether or not we use the gift and let Jesus' love shine through us to all who need Him.

It is the desire of the writer to one day meet with you, dear reader, in that place where old things have passed away and God makes everything new.

Made in the USA
Middletown, DE
22 May 2023

31149717R00111